Boarlander Boss Bear

Boarlander Boss Bear
ISBN-13: 978-1530968879
ISBN-10: 1530968879
Copyright © 2016, T. S. Joyce
First electronic publication: January 2016

T. S. Joyce
www.tsjoycewrites.wordpress.com

All Rights Are Reserved. No part of this book may be used or reproduced in any manner whatsoever without written permission, except in the case of brief quotations embodied in critical articles and reviews. The unauthorized reproduction or distribution of this copyrighted work is illegal. No part of this book may be scanned, uploaded or distributed via the Internet or any other means, electronic or print, without the author's permission.

NOTE FROM THE AUTHOR:
This book is a work of fiction. The names, characters, places, and incidents are products of the writer's imagination or have been used fictitiously and are not to be construed as real. Any resemblance to persons, living or dead, actual events, locale or organizations is entirely coincidental. The author does not have any control over and does not assume any responsibility for third-party websites or their content.

Published in the United States of America

First digital publication: January 2016
First print publication: April 2016

Boarlander Boss Bear

(Boarlander Bears, Book 1)

T. S. Joyce

ONE

Audrey Foster blew out a trembling breath and gripped the steering wheel of her old Jeep in a choke hold. She was panicking, sure, but she was about to meet the man she'd been talking to online for the last two months, and she *really* liked him.

There was a hundred percent chance she was going to screw this up.

A long snarl rattled her throat, and she gritted her teeth against the shameful sound. She couldn't mess this up because she was out of options. Her last opportunity for happiness rested with the alpha of the Boarlander crew.

Shaking her leg in quick succession, Audrey withdrew the printed picture from her sun visor and clutched it in both hands. He was so handsome. Too handsome, which was why it didn't make any sense for a badass, brawler bear shifter like Harrison Lang to ask her to come to Saratoga to meet him in person.

She couldn't breathe. Desperately, she rolled down the window and pressed herself back against the seat. Eyes tightly closed, she blew out a puff of air and wished she was braver. She'd been given the wrong animal, and now she was going into a crew of growly grizzlies who had much more control over their inner monsters than she did.

He was going to be so disappointed.

No. She could do this. Little by little, her lungs relaxed enough to let her drag in a full breath. He'd been talking to her almost every day and seemed to genuinely like her. He'd asked her to come here, wanted her closer, wanted to see her face in person, wanted to hug her, and shifters weren't supposed to lie. Or something.

Before she could change her mind, she yanked the handle of her Jeep and shoved the door open, then slid out. Her mini dress rode up her thighs, and she had to rush to smooth the tight material back down over her butt cheeks. At least no one in the long line that stretched around the corner of Sammy's Bar seemed to have noticed her bout of public indecency.

For a small town, Saratoga's only bar sure was busy. She was from a town so tiny it was practically deemed a village, and the bar in Buffalo Gap only hosted a maximum of three people at once. She knew because when the bartender wanted to take vacations, she'd filled in for him. But as a man stumbled out of the front door of Sammy's, the inside of the Saratoga bar looked filled to the brim.

"'Scuse me," she said softly to a nice looking lady with bouffant hair and smoky eye make-up who stood in the middle of the line. "Are they not letting people in?" Harrison was waiting for her inside, and she was going to be late meeting him.

"Oh, honey, are you a tourist, too? Girl, you should've Googled Sammy's before you showed up. You have to get in line early on Shifter Night."

"Shifter Night?"

The woman adjusted her oversized purse to her other arm and smacked her gum. "Yeah, every Thursday night is Shifter Night. The single bear shifters get to drink free, so if you want to meet one of their fine asses, this is the best shot you'll get. And the bears are drinking tonight," she said with a wink. "Sometimes they don't show up, and the tourists go without ever catching a glimpse of a real shifter, but tonight is your lucky night. Well, if you can get in, that is."

"Oh," Audrey said, frowning at the line that snaked around the corner. "Thank you."

"Sure, sugar. Good luck," she called as Audrey stepped carefully across the gravel toward the front of the line.

"No cuts!" a tall woman yelled as she passed.

Audrey hunched under the harshness of her voice but ignored her. There was a bouncer holding the pheromone-riddled, perfume-spritzed mob of women at bay.

"Good evening," she said politely. Her dad had always said she could catch more flies with honey than vinegar.

The bouncer was a tall fellow with a chest so muscular his tits were probably bigger than hers. He dragged his gaze down her, pausing on her curves before he looked her in the eye. Gross. "You look fuckable enough, but back of the line."

"I'm supposed to meet Harrison Lang here tonight."

The bouncer, *Ray*, his nametag read, pointed to the long line of women. "So are they."

"But Harrison and I are...dating. Online." Geez, that sounded weird.

He turned his attention to a tall man who approached with a dark-haired pregnant woman on his arm. "Hey, go on in."

The tall stranger turned an inhumanly bright green gaze on her. He definitely smelled dominant, and unable to help herself, Audrey took a healthy step backward.

"What are you?" Green Eyes asked.

"Beaston," his woman admonished. "You can't ask people that."

Beaston angled his head and narrowed his eyes. "Don't all that perfume shit give you a headache?"

"Y-yes."

"Then why wear it?"

To hide what I am. She couldn't drag the words out of her throat, so she stood there awkwardly, unable to think of a single good excuse. He would hear a lie anyway. She'd heard about Beaston. The dark-haired woman tugging at his hand must be Aviana, registered raven shifter and member of the Gray Back crew. Audrey's nervousness jacked up to the sky. She was among beasts now.

"Harrison's girl?" Beaston asked.

Failing to hold his gaze, she stared at his

scuffed work boots and nodded. "Yes."

"She's with us," Aviana told Ray.

Ray stepped closer to the dark-haired woman who cradled her stomach protectively. He lowered his voice when he argued, "But Ana—"

"She ain't lyin'," Beaston said, flashing the bouncer a dangerous glare. He pointed to his temple. "I would've heard it."

Beaston shocked Audrey to her glossy black heels when he wrapped his giant hand around hers and nearly ground her bones to dust as he dragged her into the bar behind him and Aviana. The second they were in the door, he released her, and she subtly shook her hand out. Mother fluffer, he was strong and none-to-gentle, and now she had even more respect for Aviana. If a raven could survive a bear shifter like Beaston, she had some mountainous inner strength.

"Just so you know," Beaston said, lifting his chin. "You don't make no sense."

"Beaston," Aviana admonished. She watched her mate walk away and then gave Audrey an apologetic look. "Manners aren't his strong suit."

"It's okay." Audrey rubbed her throbbing hand. "I don't make sense to me, either."

Aviana's lips curved into a smile, and she cocked her head. The woman gave one deliberate blink, and Audrey smiled. Even if she hadn't known Aviana was a raven shifter, she would've guessed she was some kind of bird from her mannerisms.

"I'm Aviana Novak." She held her fine-boned hand out for a shake. Sometimes Audrey didn't know her strength so she was deliberately gentle, but she didn't need to be. Aviana gripped her in a surprisingly strong grasp before releasing her.

"I'm Audrey Foster."

"Harrison's over at the bar, but Clinton is a mega-cock-blocker so...good luck with that one."

Audrey huffed a nervous laugh. "Thanks."

Ana gave her a little wave, cradled the swell of her belly in her hands, and made her way gracefully through the crowd toward a table in the back.

One look around, and it was apparent Audrey was smack-dab in the middle of the all-stars of Damon's mountains. Cora Keller of the Breck Crew had an entire page on her pro-shifter website dedicated to the bears, falcons, ravens, gorillas, and dragons of Saratoga.

Kong, a dark-headed, barrel-chested titan

gorilla shifter was working behind the bar with his mate, Layla. A few of the Ashe Crew were playing darts and pool against the back wall, and the Beck brothers were playing a country song on the stage. They were damn good. And as Aviana had said, Harrison and his Boarlanders seemed to be taking up space at the bar.

Her heart pounded faster as she saw him in person for the first time. Harrison's powerful legs were splayed and locked as he stood talking to one of Kong's Lowlanders, Kirk, another gorilla shifter. She was going to have to build up some major courage to approach her man while he was in the middle of a conversation with a big, dominant silverback.

Maybe she should take a shot before she talked to Harrison. Beaston was glaring at her from the corner with the calculating look of a predator judging how fast he would need to run to cut her off at the legs. *Eeek.* Audrey ducked his unsettling gaze and strode for the bar. Harrison was waiting for her, and stalling wouldn't fix her nerves. She was growing more cowardly with every second of hesitation.

Her high heels felt sticky on the wood

floors with each step, and as a tipsy woman turned and sloshed her cranberry drink right next to Audrey, she understood why. This place was probably next to impossible to keep clean until after hours.

Harrison wore a dark blue T-shirt that was thin enough to show every ripple of muscle in his back as he reached for a drink Kong set in front of him. His shoulders were as wide as a barn, and his back was shaped like a V, the sexiest damned letter of the alphabet.

Audrey wiped her clammy palms on her dress, inching it down toward her knees with the motion. This was the most scandalous thing she'd ever worn. What if Harrison didn't like short dresses?

Stop it. Everything will be fine.

She waited politely behind him as Kirk asked, "And you're sure you need help this badly?" His dark eyebrows arched high. "It seems extreme."

"Yeah, well, I have an asshole bear who has chased off half my damned crew, and you don't seem intimidated by Clinton, so yeah, I need your help. If Kong can spare you, I'd really appreciate it. Just until logging season is over, then I'll look for more cutters." He cast a blond-haired man sitting a few seats away a pissed-off glance. "I can't just bring anyone in. He'll bleed 'em." He lowered his voice and muttered, "Fuckin' Beaston junior."

She wouldn't have heard him without her oversensitive hearing, and apparently she wasn't the only one listening because the Clinton in question twirled his wrist and gave Harrison his middle finger and then an empty smile.

Audrey worked hard to swallow the growl in her throat. She didn't know Clinton, but from the way he looked at Harrison, she didn't much care for him. She'd clenched her fists unintentionally, so she relaxed them, took a steadying breath, and poked Harrison on the shoulder. She jammed her finger on his rock hard muscles and flinched back. Between him and Beaston, her hand was going to be mangled by the morning.

Harrison gave her a look over his shoulder, locked eyes with her, and froze. God, he was a beautiful man. If she saw him on the street, she would think he was some model instead of the alpha of a notoriously rough-and-tumble grizzly crew. His strong jaw was shaved smooth, so she could glide her attention over every appealing curve of his face. He turned slowly, lifting his chin and trapping her completely with his gaze. She'd thought from the pictures that his eye color was dark, a soft brown maybe, but in person, they were a stormy blue color. Straightening his spine, he stood to his full height as he squared up to her, and Audrey arched her neck back to hold his enchanting gaze. Holy heaven, he was a mountain. His nostrils flared slightly, and whatever he smelled caused a frown to mar his dark brows. His T-shirt hugged his muscular arms as he crossed them over his chest, and tonight, he'd worn his hair different than his pictures. It was shorter on the sides and styled longer on top.

"Did you get a haircut?" she asked lamely.

His steel blue eyes narrowed. "Not lately."

"Oh. Well, I like it." She tried to smile, but it fell off her face immediately with a nervous twitch.

"Did you need something?"

Confused, she said, "It's me. Audrey."

His eyebrows lifted, and he shot Kirk a quick glance, then held out his hand to her. "Nice to meet you."

"Yeah, finally, right?"

Harrison froze mid-handshake and pursed his lips into a thin line. "Okay then."

"That's bear-speak for 'vamoose,'" Clinton

offered helpfully from down the bar.

"Shut the *fuck* up," Harrison growled, apparently good and done with Clinton for some reason.

"Uh, can I buy you a drink?" she asked Clinton, who was slurping loudly on his straw.

"It's Shifter Night. I drink for free," he said in a tone that said he thought she was the stupidest breathing organism on the planet.

Audrey curled her lips over her teeth before she could stop her inner animal and choked back yet another growl. She would be forced to Change soon.

Harrison took a step back and sat on the stool, looked at her dress and heels, then rubbed his hand on his smooth jaw. "Do you want a drink, Audrey?"

Clinton slapped his hand on the countertop. "Harrison, as Second—"

A ferocious snarl came from Harrison's chest as he offered Clinton a death glare. "Not Second yet. You and Bash haven't worked that out, and even if you were, you're still not alpha. You reached for the crown and missed. Go ahead and piss me off some more tonight, Clinton. I'll send you back to the Gray Backs so fast your fuckin' head will spin."

"You wouldn't—"

"Don't test me." Harrison's eyes were a much brighter blue now, and Audrey hadn't been able to draw a breath since Clinton had first spoken. The air was simply unbreathable. It filled her lungs like tar and froze her in place. Beaston had been dominant, but Harrison…Harrison was a monster.

Clinton dropped his gaze like a smart bear since Harrison looked like he was about to commit murder.

"Maybe I should come back later," she whispered. Nope, getting in the middle of a bear fight was not how she'd seen this going.

"Sit. Please." Harrison gestured to the bar stool between him and Kirk.

She was going to pass out if she didn't get more oxygen to her body, and soon.

"You're suffocating me, man," Kirk said low.

Harrison cut off his growl, and the heaviness lifted. With one last fiery glance at Clinton, Harrison lifted a finger to the pretty blond bartender. "Layla, can I get a beer for the lady? Put it on a tab for me, will you?" His voice was way too gravelly, but at least his words were polite.

"Hallelujah, Harrison's buying a lady a drink," Layla muttered as she reached into the fridge for a beer. "Jake is going to crap his pants with happiness."

She shouldn't have heard that last part because of the noisy bar patrons around her, but for the first time in her life, Audrey was glad she had heightened senses. Apparently, Harrison didn't buy many women drinks. Good.

"Hare-Bear," a dolled up woman Audrey's age whined from her group of buxom beauty friends. "I've been asking you to buy me a drink for a month straight. What makes her so special?"

Harrison's profile was rigid as he rolled his eyes heavenward and strangled his half-full beer bottle.

"You'll break it and cut your hand," Audrey murmured, gently prying the glass from his grip.

He shot her a wary glare, but let it go easily enough. "Why do you care?"

"Because I like you." Silly man, she'd told him that a dozen times already. Or rather, typed it to him.

"I would heal. Shifters do that, you know."

She opened her mouth to respond, but Layla set the beer in front of her and gave a polite smile. The bartender shoved a laminated flyer over the counter to Audrey. *Shifter Facts* was typed in big neon letters across the top of a long list. "Jake takes Shifter Night super seriously." Layla pointed to a bullet point explaining how fast shifters can heal from injuries, a fact Audrey knew first-hand.

"You wear a lot of perfume," Harrison said, eyeing her as he took a swig of his beer.

Audrey choked down a gulp of the nasty drink and stifled the urge to barf. Beer wasn't her favorite unless it tasted like a fruit— something she'd explained to Harrison as they'd joked back and forth online. Maybe he was testing her.

She hadn't exactly told him what she was yet because, well, telling people about her inner animal usually caused them to flee. And if she was honest, she still wasn't ready to tell Harrison, even though she was actually looking him in the face after two months of bonding. Being a shifter was a secret she liked to keep as hidden as she could. Perfume masked the scent of her fur, and from the confused look on Harrison's face, it was working like a gem. She choked down another swig. "So good," she rasped out.

"What kinda girl doesn't like beer?"

Harrison asked.

"Hare-Bear," the groupie called again from much closer. She slid her arms over his shoulders and rested her cheek between his shoulder blades, a possessive smile on her face as she glared at Audrey.

"Get off him before I rip those ridiculous eyelashes off," Audrey said blandly, her hands clenched on the bar top.

Harrison snorted but didn't move to shake off the woman. Her inner beasty was snarling to rip out of her skin and filet the handsy woman.

"I like beer," Eyelashes purred.

"If I give you my leftovers, will you leave?" Audrey asked, sliding her beer across the counter toward her.

"No thanks. I don't want herpes."

"Well, it would only be fair since you've probably given me, like, six airborne STDs since you've wandered over here."

"Both of y'all are going home without a werebear dick," Clinton offered through an empty smile. "Might as well retract the claws."

Harrison heaved a sigh. "Holly, get off."

"I'm trying to," she whispered against his ear. Her painted red lips puckered against his earlobe, and *that was enough*.

"Whoa," Kirk said, gripping Audrey's arm before she poured her beer on the skank's head.

Harrison cracked an amused grin, hesitated, then turned and cupped the back of Audrey's head. His eyes flashed with challenge the second before he leaned in and pressed his lips to hers.

"Asshole!" Holly shrieked. The sound of her heels clacking away allowed Audrey to relax into the kiss.

Harrison eased back to end it, but she had wanted this so badly since the day he'd first responded to her message on the matchmaking site. Standing between his legs, hand resting on his powerful thigh, she chased his mouth with hers and slid her palm up to his chest. He gripped the back of her neck and angled his face, deepening the kiss, and if she wasn't careful, she was going to purr and give herself away. His tongue brushed the seam of her lips as she nestled in between his legs. Audrey parted for him and let off a tiny moan as she tasted him. She was soaring, her body going numb everywhere except where they touched. Harrison's arm snaked around her back, and he dragged her closer as he pushed his tongue into her mouth again. God, he could kiss!

But then he pulled away abruptly, searching her eyes. She felt utterly dazed from his kiss, but he looked alarmed, and his heartbeat was pounding where she'd rested her hand on his strong chest.

"Who are you?" he demanded.

Silly man playing silly games. Audrey smiled, so happy and relieved he was even better in person than online. "I'm your mate."

TWO

Audrey whats-her-name had lost her damned mind. Or maybe she'd never had it to begin with. Her voice was completely honest as she'd uttered those words. *I'm your mate.* What the hell?

"I beg to differ," Clinton said from way too close.

"Back off, man," Harrison gritted out. He released his grip on Audrey's body. He'd been holding her too tight, but the scrawny little human didn't even bat an eye. Maybe she had high pain tolerance. If she knew how riled up she had gotten his bear with her little fifteen second French kiss, she would've been running for the hills. He wanted to take her in the back office and bend her over Jake's desk. Or he had until she had shown her crazy.

He was no one's mate. Never was, never

would be.

Her perfume was making him dizzy, so he shook his head hard and stood. He needed to get away from her. She was fogging his mind. He'd kissed her to piss Clinton and Holly off, but he hadn't expected to get lost in it. That wasn't what he did. He was the careful one. The collected one. He had to be in order to bear the pain of losing his crew one by one. Clinton had done that, chased everyone off. Maybe that was why he'd lost his control with this woman. He had finally started to show how badly he was hurting. Shit. He needed to get out of here, far away from the gorgeous brunette with the thick southern accent and the curves for days. Fucking sexy, tight dress...and those legs. Heels. He'd never liked the spiky shoes before, but on Audrey he wanted them lying on the floor of his trailer.

She was bewitching him. He was vulnerable, cracking, breaking, and she was here clawing her way into his head and making him feel much drunker than he actually was.

"What's wrong?" She looked worried, and genuine concern tainted her words.

"I don't know you," he gritted out.

Her face fell. "Don't say that. Please. I'm

the same as I've always been."

"Lady, I don't even understand what you're talking about. I've never seen you before tonight, and you're acting way too familiar."

"You tell her," Clinton said like a fucking cheerleader.

Harrison wanted to break his neck, but instead, he pulled his wallet from his pocket and threw down a ten dollar bill for Layla.

"Why are you acting like this? I don't understand what I did wrong. You were the one who asked me to come here."

"No, I didn't. I've never met you before tonight."

She looked so utterly confused, she must be mental. She really thought they had some kind of rapport, some kind of relationship. Groupies were aggressive sometimes, but this was different. All the beauty in the world didn't matter if she was a nutcase. She reached for him, and he stepped out of range. God, he wanted her to touch him again, but she wasn't safe. Audrey was a danger to him and his crew. "Clinton, if you don't wipe that smile off your face, I'm going to pitch you off a mountain."

"No women at the trailer park. That's the rule," the asshole sang.

"I don't understand," Audrey said, and now her pretty brown eyes were brimming with moisture.

He wanted to retch but didn't know why. He hadn't drank that much.

His bear was scratching at his skin, and he was in serious danger of an uncontrolled Change. "I have to go." Harrison ripped his gaze away from her pretty pursed lips and wove through the crowd. With every step away from her, his stomach hurt worse. She was a witch or…something.

"Harrison?" she asked from behind him. Her voice sounded so hurt. So disappointed.

Clenching his hands, he shoved the door open and escaped into the night. Only the farther he got away from the witch, the worse he felt. Gripping the tailgate of his truck, he dragged in a lungful of cool air. After a minute of focusing on the long line of women waiting outside of Sammy's, he turned over his palms and stared at his shaking hands.

He wasn't hers. He didn't belong to anyone.

Whatever that woman was doing to him, it was dangerous—not only for him and his crew, but for her as well. Shifter groupies thought they wanted a piece of him, but they didn't really understand the danger. He was an alpha, and one who was reeling and struggling to keep a crew under him.

And Audrey, that crazy, little, fragile human had no business teasing a wounded predator.

THREE

She'd been duped.

Audrey didn't know how or why yet, but she'd been tricked into coming all the way out to Wyoming for a man who didn't exist.

Unless…

Maybe this was Harrison's way of keeping their relationship casual. Or maybe he didn't like the way she looked in person. Or maybe he didn't like her accent, perfume, nail color, smile… There were a billion things that could've made him decide to pretend he'd never talked to her before. But if that was his game, he was extraordinarily good at it because his eyes had been so solemn and shocked, and his tone so honest. *I've never met you before.*

The thought of last night's meeting made her double over the steering wheel with embarrassment. She'd never said the word *mate* out loud, and clearly, she'd used it wrong.

It sucked being a shifter, stuck between the human and supernatural worlds, and fitting in with neither.

Audrey turned down the country station on the radio and spread the crinkled map across the steering wheel. Even if her cell phone had gotten good reception in the valleys between the towering mountains that surrounded her, the GPS had basically laughed at her when she'd entered in *Boarland Mobile Park*.

She understood the need to live out away from people like Harrison and his crew did. It was easier to Change without people knowing, watching, asking questions, judging…hating. As she maneuvered the final switchback and turned onto a gravel road, she was struck by how beautiful this place was. Some of the trees were dead and brown, but a majority of the evergreens here stood tall and strong with rich green needles that painted the landscape in a myriad of earthy colors. Audrey reached out the open window and let the crisp breeze run through her fingertips. She lived out in the country in Texas, but the landscape didn't touch this. Thorny mesquite trees didn't hold a candle to the hill country she found herself in now. It was May, and sunny, and the sounds of cicadas and birds were a constant song here.

She rode the brake and slowed down as the entrance to the trailer park came into view. Across the road, there was a massive, arched sign that read *Boarland Mobile Park*. Only that had been crossed out in bright red paint, and over it was written *Missionary Impossible*.

What did that mean?

The second she laid eyes on the destroyed park, she regretted showing up uninvited. There were six ancient trailers, lined up three in a row on either side of the road, and settled lengthways. The dingy white paint was chipped on each, and the roof shingles were years over good use. Entire sheets of disintegrating shingles had fallen off one trailer and lay on top of the overgrown landscaping that looked to be the biggest mutant weeds she'd ever seen in her life. Some would be taller than her if she got the mind to stand beside them. There were three sun-bleached, plastic flamingos toppled over in one of the weed-riddled yards, and a plethora of old tractor parts sat in a pile at the end of the trailer park. Two rusty old cars were up on blocks and looked like they hadn't been worked on in years, and instead of a door, one of the singlewide mobile homes had a stack of old tires in front of it. The road was made of gravel that had washed out, and various potholes tried to swallow her Jeep before she pulled to a stop in front of a giant anthill that had been built in the middle of the road.

This place looked like an abandoned ghost town. Or at least, it would've looked like one if Clinton wasn't sitting in a duct-taped, plastic lawn chair at the end of the road, drinking a beer and glaring at her. He wore a trucker hat, aviator sunglasses, a white T-shirt two sizes too small and the tiniest pair of yellow shorts she'd ever seen on a man. Yellow and white baseball socks clad his hairy legs up to his knees. He wore old sneakers and had shaved the facial scruff he'd worn yesterday into an 80s style mustache. God, this was weird.

She cut the engine and got out, but as she opened her mouth to say a polite greeting, he lifted a finger to shush her, bent over his creaking chair, then pulled an old metal sign out of the dirt beside him. In exceptionally shitty handwriting, it read *no girls allowed in the trailer park*.

Fantastic.

"I came to talk to Harrison," she said in a voice that sounded tired, even to herself.

"Girl!" someone yelled from one of the trailers, startling her.

The tires in the doorway of the nearest trailer toppled over, and a giant, behemoth of a man scrambled over the make-shift door he'd just gladiator-kicked down. "Oh, my God, there's a girl. In the park!" He jammed a finger at Clinton. "I swear if you screw this up for me, I'll bleed you, Gray Back."

"Don't call me that!" Clinton yelled. "And she ain't even here for you, Bash. She's here for Harrison."

The dark-haired titan with the bright green eyes pointed both index fingers at her with a big grin on his face. "I'm gonna make you pizza rolls. You want wine? I have, like, six boxes of wine. Don't leave!" He turned to rush back inside, but spun at the door. Pressing his hand to his chest, he arched his dark eyebrows and slowed down. "I'm Sebastian, but everyone calls me Bash. I'm gonna feed you now." He kicked a wayward tire out of the way and disappeared into his trailer.

"I'm Audrey!" she called after him.

"Nice to meet you, Audrey!" Bash called in

a muffled voice.

"Where is the rest of your crew?" she asked Clinton.

Clinton gave her a feral smile. "I chased 'em off."

She narrowed her eyes at him and leaned against the front of her Jeep. "You won't be chasing me off. I'm only here to sort out what happened with Harrison, and then I'll be headed back to Texas."

"I love Texas," Bash called from inside of his trailer.

"I don't," Clinton muttered, crossing his arms.

"Have you ever been there?"

"No."

Bash wrestled his kitchen window open. "I've been three times. Pretty girls, big hair, and southern manners. I bet you say 'thank you' and 'you're welcome' and help old ladies across the street and shit."

"Uuuh, yes, but I don't think that's just a Texas thing. I think that's a decent person thing."

"Right." Bash smiled vacantly, then disappeared into the dark kitchen.

"Sooo," she drawled out. "Where's Harrison?"

"Everyone says I'm the fucked-up bear who belongs in the Gray Backs," Clinton said, angling his head. "But maybe I'm the normal one."

"I don't know what that means."

"Harrison is patrolling the boundaries of Boarlander property. Do you want to know why?"

"Sure."

"Because he don't sleep. He don't feel safe. His bear won't settle unless—"

"Clinton!" Harrison barked out from the tree line between two trailers. "Stop talking. Now." He was clad in only a low-slung pair of jeans with holes at the knees. As pretty as his eyes were right now, all bright and the color of a summer sky, that wasn't what held her attention. He had the face of an angel, yes, but his body had been mangled. His entire torso was rippling with muscle and covered in scars, both from claws and what looked like about a dozen bullet holes. She took a step closer to the door of her Jeep.

"You know the rules, *alpha*," Clinton gritted out. "No girls in the—"

Harrison opened his mouth and roared so loud it shook the ground beneath her feet. It was horrifying to hear such a feral noise from a man.

Clinton stood and chucked the sign into the woods like a Frisbee. "I challenge you for alpha."

"You just challenged me yesterday, asshole!" Harrison bellowed.

"You're failing to uphold your own damned rules. That's weak, Harrison. Change!"

Harrison hooked his hands on his hips and glared at Audrey. He let off a long sigh that tapered into a terrifying snarl. "Get in your car and leave."

"I have something to talk to you about."

Clinton was stripping out of his eighties-style clothes and grumbling about how, "I have to do everything around here."

Harrison scrubbed his hand down his face, and his eyes blazed even brighter. "Lady—"

"Audrey."

Another growl. "Audrey. This is no place for you, and we have nothing to say to each other." His attention flickered to her Jeep, then to her face, then he frowned at the back window, which was still rolled halfway down. "What did you do to your seats?"

She grimaced and wished she'd remembered to roll her windows back up when she'd stopped. The real story was she'd

Changed accidentally in her ride and shredded the seats in her fury at being trapped. "An animal got in there," she murmured, sticking as close to the truth as she could.

Clinton was stripping out of his pants now, and when he was through, he angled his face from side to side, stretching his neck, or popping it perhaps. He bounced around, punching at the air.

"Again?" Bash asked from the open doorway where he held a red plastic cup of what smelled like un-fine wine. "Clinton, he's bested you three times this week."

"I'm like the little engine that could," Clinton growled, eyes on his alpha.

Bash shook his head. "Audrey, you should take cover." He sounded so disappointed, so sad.

"I don't want you to fight." She was panicking that this was somehow because of her. Harrison was already covered in scars, and this really wasn't how she'd imagined this place would be. She'd thought it would be like happy-go-lucky shifter land, but it was dark, gritty, and the bears fought too much.

Harrison spat on the ground and unbuttoned his jeans. "If I win, no more alpha challenges. This is for everything." He said it quietly enough, but the impact of his words was instant on Clinton.

"You won't challenge me back if I win?"

Harrison shook his head slow as he shoved his jeans down and kicked out of them. Harrison was all smooth rippling muscles, overlaid with a patchwork of scars that made him look dangerously beautiful. Warmth filled her stomach the moment she laid eyes on his long dick, swinging between his legs.

"Oh, my goodness, that's your dick." Audrey scrunched up her nose. "You're naked." *Stop. Talking!*

Harrison ghosted her a bright-eyed glance. "Get in the Jeep."

"I'm not leaving."

"Just get in there until this is through. I don't want you hurt."

"Oh." She scrambled inside but didn't roll up the window. Not yet.

"If I win," he said to Clinton, who was now pacing across the road, "no more challenges. You aren't dominant enough to hold this crew. If you want to be alpha so badly, you'll find another."

"Deal."

Harrison flinched inward, and an instant later, a massive, dark-furred grizzly bruin exploded from his skin. A wave of power passed through Audrey's window and over her skin, lifting the fine hairs on her body with chills. She couldn't take her eyes off him as he charged the blond grizzly. They crashed with the force of an avalanche. Roaring, clawing, and slapping echoed through the valley. Clinton's impossibly long canines flashed in the instant before he sank them into the muscular hump between Harrison's shoulder blades, but the dark brawler hooked his arm around Clinton and slammed him to the ground. In a flurry of violence, his teeth were on Clinton's neck, and the blond bear froze underneath him. Harrison held him there, the promise of death in his eyes. So easily, he could rip Clinton's throat out. So easily, he could end his life, but he didn't. Instead, he released him and walked away with long, powerful strides. He stood on his hind legs and roared, then shrank back into his human skin. He walked right past her Jeep and into the first trailer in the park.

Audrey sat there plastered to her seat, too shocked to move or breathe as Clinton transformed into his human body again and spat red onto the white gravel road. He gave her a death glare, then pushed himself up and limped into one of the trailers at the end of the road.

When she dared a look to the side, Bash was standing there leaned against her window, slurping a pizza roll straight off a paper plate.

She startled hard and gasped. How had she, with her heightened senses, not noticed him approach?

"You wear a lot of perfume," he said casually, like he hadn't just watched his crew go to battle. "Smells like flowers and pesticide."

"Thank you?"

"I knew it. Texas manners."

"It's really not just Texas—"

"Pizza roll?" He held the paper plate through the window.

Out of politeness, she took one and smiled.

"Say it," he urged through a bright grin.

With a sigh, she muttered, "Thank you."

"You're welcome." Bash arched his eyebrows and nodded, apparently proud of himself. "My dick is even bigger than Harrison's."

"Okay, I'm going to go talk to him now," she said, pushing the door open.

"By like a centimeter probably, but it

counts as bigger."

Her cheeks were on fire as she ducked her gaze and sidled around the Jeep at a fast clip. She didn't bother knocking on Harrison's closed door but, instead, let herself in to escape Bash, who was following close behind.

"I like your hair," he rushed out as she closed the door behind her.

She pressed her back against the door and tried to adjust her eyes to the darkness. Apparently Harrison was fine with his trailer looking like a cave.

The only light filtered in through an open window over his kitchen sink. The *riiip* of first-aid packaging sounded from where Harrison stood with his profile to her in front of the sink.

"What are you doing here?" he asked in a low, snarly voice.

The air was too thick in his den. "Is it always like this for you?"

"Like what?"

"Violent? Unsettled? Cora Keller's website said you had seven bears under you, and that dominance was already established."

"Well, Cora's updates didn't include Clinton. It takes one bad apple to spoil the bunch." Harrison inhaled deeply and tried to press a wash cloth over the puncture wounds on his back, but the injury was out of reach.

She couldn't stand this. The light switch made a single *click* under her fingertip. She padded into the kitchen, then took the soaking cloth from him. As she dabbed the blood from the puncture wounds on his back, she asked, "And Clinton is that bad apple?"

"Yes." Harrison gripped the edge of the sink and sighed. "No, that's not fair of me. He's just spiraling, and he's taking the rest of us with him. I didn't know what I was getting myself into when I accepted him after he left the Gray Backs. I didn't realize how much shit Creed put up with to manage troubled bears. He's better than me at this." Harrison turned and ticked up a sad smile, just there and gone in a moment. "The Boarlanders are the new C-team now."

His eyes were still too bright, but he didn't feel as heavy anymore, and the feral lines of his face had relaxed.

Audrey dropped her gaze and fidgeted with the damp cloth. "You won't need bandages. The bite mark is already closed up." She dared a glance to the bullet scars on his torso. "Were you shot?"

Harrison grabbed her wrist and stopped

her from touching one. When had she reached for him?

"Sorry," she whispered.

"Say your piece and be done, Audrey. Like I told you, this isn't the place for you."

Or it was the exact kind of place for her.

Audrey reached into her back pocket and pulled out a folded stack of papers she'd printed off at the hotel she was staying in. "This is why I'm here."

With a slight frown, Harrison released her wrist and accepted the papers. He unfolded them carefully and read the first page and then the second, his frown deepening. "I don't understand. I didn't write any of this."

"Yeah, I figured that out. So, you probably thought I was crazy last night, but to me, I'd come all the way here to finally meet a man I'd fallen for. A man who is obviously not you."

"Worms," he murmured absently. His eyes narrowed to slits as he read from a column of their online conversation. "Fake Harrison talked to you about different kinds of worms."

"Yeah, that was a weird conversation."

His chest rattled with a soft growl, and he clutched the paperwork tightly in his fist. "I think I know who did this. I'm sorry you got caught up in whatever is happening, but I didn't have anything to do with you coming here."

"Yeah." Her eyes burned with how badly she'd been taken advantage of. "I know. I just feel pretty stupid. I spent most of my savings to get here. And then I still have these feelings for you because yours is the picture I saw all this time we were fake-dating, and it's hard telling my heart to stop feeling."

"Audrey," he drawled, but she hated the pity in his voice so she rushed onward.

"I know whoever did this isn't anything like you. I realized that last night. This person is talkative and outgoing, and you seem to have a lot going on right now that makes you quiet and a little reckless."

"Reckless how?"

"The kiss."

Harrison ran his hand over his hair and stared down at the papers in his hand. "Oh, that."

"Full disclosure—that was the best kiss I've ever had, by a lot, and it made all this even more confusing."

"Bangaboarlander.com," he read as he narrowed his eyes at the logo on the paperwork. "Why were you on this website, anyway? You're a nice woman, a beautiful woman." He jerked his chin toward his kitchen window. "You don't want this life, Audrey. You could have something normal with a regular human man."

Sadness tugging at her heart, Audrey smiled. She'd tried and failed epically at that. "Yeah, well, I just wanted to explain the mix-up before I left town. I didn't want to be the story you told years from now about the crazy lady who thought she was your instant mate." Audrey set the washcloth on the counter. "It was nice to meet you, Harrison."

"I'm sorry I wasn't what you expected," he rushed out just as she was about to walk through the front door.

Audrey gripped the knob. "Well, that's part of the problem. You were better."

His eyes were glowing in the dim lighting, and she committed to memory the vision of him in this exact moment. Beautiful, dominant, powerful, scarred-up shifter. He could've been a match for her animal, but he wasn't invested in the relationship like she was.

"Goodbye, Harrison."

"Bye," he murmured in a dazed voice.

And as she made her way down his sagging porch stairs, she blinked back tears. Now would be the hard part. Now she would have to go back to Texas feeling emptier than when she'd left.

Now she would have to rip her heart away from the stranger who had stolen it.

FOUR

Harrison gritted his teeth against yet another bone-deep wave of anger and grabbed the stack of papers from the front seat. He shoved his pickup door open and made his way across the gravel road of the Grayland Mobile Park toward where the alpha, Creed, was working on a bobcat near the edge of the clearing.

The Gray Backs were out in full force, partying around a built-in brick fire pit in the center of the trailer park. He wished Clinton wouldn't fight fixing up the Boarland Mobile Park so he could create something like this for his crew. Maybe some of them wouldn't have left if he could've done things differently and given them a place worth staying for. Any time he did repairs, though, Clinton's control faltered, and he accused Harrison of fixing it up to attract women and cubs.

"Hey," Creed greeted him as he wiped his grease-covered hands on a dirty cloth.

"I need to talk to you."

"Uh-oh," the dark-haired alpha said, leaning his elbow on the yellow machine. "That sounds bad." With a twitch of his chin at his crew, he asked, "Which one did what?"

He should definitely leave the worst for last with Creed. "First, I wanted to know if I could syphon some help from you. My cutters are just a skeleton crew now, and I can't keep up with the jobsites if I don't get some help. Kong is giving me Kirk until the end of logging season, but I need at least one more able body in order to get the trees cut before you and the Ashe Crew start."

"Oh, shit. How many do you have left?"

"Clinton and Bash."

Creed took a step back and drew up straight. "Holy hell, Harrison. How are you still upright? Losing one member is hard, but you lost most of your damned crew. Why did they leave?"

"Liam left to move closer to the mother of his kid so he could share custody, Darin met a girl out of state and followed her, and the rest...well, you know."

"Clinton?"

"He's killing me, man. I don't know how you put up with his shit."

"He wasn't so bad when I had him. Sure, he was a pain about girls coming into the trailer park, but when we started pairing up, he ran to your crew. He's acting bad now because he doesn't have anywhere else to go. He fled two crews before he came to me."

"Do you know what's wrong with him?"

Creed looked sick. "Yeah part of it, and it's his story to share. It's not my place to tell you."

"Don't worry about it, man. I get it. That stuff's personal. I'm not the alpha he needs, or he would've opened up to me sooner. Instead, he's focused on pushing every bear out of the Boarlanders. Hell, he's challenged me for alpha four times this week. If he gets to Bash, I don't know what I'll do."

"Kick him out then. Or put him down."

"Creed," Harrison said through a frown. "That's fucked up, man."

"And do you think any other alpha would've put up with having his crew pushed out? How many bonds have you had to break to get to skeleton crew status? That's poison right there, Harrison. Any other alpha would've cut him off or put him down."

"Would you?"

Creed dragged his dark gaze to his crew of misfits and scratched his jaw with his thumbnail. "No," he admitted low. "Clinton had potential when he lived here."

"And do you still think he does?"

"I'm not his alpha anymore, Harrison. It's not my call. It's yours." Creed crossed his arms over his chest and stared thoughtfully at his crew who were joking and laughing near a table stacked with odd-looking food.

The breeze shifted and Harrison nearly retched. Whatever they were feasting on stunk like hell.

"Look," Creed continued, "all my bears are mated and working on families. They won't move to your crew even temporarily without bringing their mates, and Clinton won't do well with that. The only floater I have is Mason, and I can tell you right now, he's hunting for a mate. He won't follow your bullshit rule about no women at your trailer park, so if you want him, you'll have to lift that. He deserves to find someone."

"Yeah, Kong told me the same about Kirk, and Bash's bear is ready for a mate, too. Clinton is going to lose his shit."

"Let him. He's made his problem all of your

problem for too long. It's tough love time, and if he doesn't like it, he can run, just like he always does."

"To where? There's no more bachelor crews around here."

"That's not your problem. That's his. Mason is in town right now, but I'll ask him to help your crew out this season as soon as he gets back."

"I sure appreciate it, man."

"No problem. I don't even know how you're still sane after breaking bonds, so I'll help however I can until you get your crew back on its feet."

"If I can."

"You will. If I can get those idiots to get along," Creed said, gesturing to the Gray Backs, "you can handle the Boarlanders. You want to say hi to Georgia while you're here? She's been bummed lately. She says you've been avoiding her when she's out on patrol."

"Shit. I didn't think she would notice." He was closer with the park ranger than any of the Gray Backs. She'd saved his life when poachers came after him, and at the cost of her humanity. She was a shifter because her mate, Jason, had Turned her to save her, but she bore the same bullet-hole scars he did.

Harrison usually checked in on her while she was on patrol around his territory, but he'd been steering clear so his shit mood wouldn't worry her. "I'll make it right, but it's not her I'm here to talk to."

Creed's eyes narrowed. "Who?"

"Your resident worm farmer."

Creed shook his head and turned back to his work on the bobcat. "No can do today, Harrison. It's bad timing."

Bad timing? Everyone looked happy enough. The Gray Backs were cracking up as they ate that atrocious-smelling food. Jason was gagging while Gia clapped him on the back and barked out a laugh. There was a big, hand-painted sign strung between two of the trailers that said *Happy Pre-Baby Party,* and the table was decorated with pink and blue balloons. Tiny, nerdy, red-headed Willa, the worm-lovin' woman herself, was sitting on a lavish, toilet-paper-decorated throne with a crown and a scepter as she ate what looked like a cracker with mustard and sardines.

"Is Willa pregnant?"

"No," Creed muttered. "She and Matt decided they are ready to try for a baby, so apparently that decision warrants a party."

Matt sat in another make-shift throne with

a huge swollen belly that Clara, Damon's mate, was covering in strips of dripping paper-mache. And as Matt took a deep swig of beer, Aviana was painting *Future Alpha* over the swell of his stomach.

"Is Matt wearing a pregnancy belly?"

"That he is. And my totally normal crew is currently eating all of the insane pregnancy cravings Willa has imagined she will have. The cake is made of capers and beans."

"Barely Alpha!" Willa called out to Creed. "Come try this banana dipped in pickle juice."

But when her eyes landed on Harrison, she said, "Eeee," stood slowly, then began tiptoeing toward her trailer.

"Bangaboarlander-dot-com," Harrison called out. "Willa, we need to talk."

"I think I'm having Braxton Hicks contractions," she called, clutching her tiny stomach.

Creed sighed an irritated sound and said, "Good God, Willa, come here."

She hunched her shoulders under his command. "Fine." She kicked gravel and pouted the entire way to Harrison. "You're going to ruin my party."

"You ruined some lady's life, Willa, so I don't have sympathy for you right now."

"What lady?" she asked too innocently as she shoved her thick glasses farther up her nose.

Harrison handed her the printed stacks of conversations Willa had with Audrey under the guise that she was actually Harrison. "Audrey showed up to Shifter Night the other day, thinking I asked her to come."

Creed yanked the papers out of Willa's hand and began to read them.

Willa's little pixie face morphed into a dastardly smile. "She showed up then?"

"Yeah, but why the hell are you running a website with fake accounts for me, Bash, and Clinton? Bash hacked your site, and it has hundreds of hits on each of our made-up profiles."

"Okay, okay, okay, I can explain. I started Bangaboarlander as a way to prank Clinton because he's a whiney B-hole. Please tell me you saw his profile."

"Yeah. Clinton Fuller, age twenty-eight, nymphomaniac, giant penis, no STDs, wants tons of kids, loves to give flowers and cuddle, immediately ready for a mate, net worth: a billion dollars. And then you listed his actual phone number."

Willa laughed, holding her belly as she

doubled over. "I love that part. Have any of his admirers called him?"

"All the damned time. He threw his phone into Bear Trap Falls the other day and then lost all control. He changed for an entire day and has been on a tear ever since."

Willa pursed her lips and stifled another round of giggles.

"This isn't funny."

But when Harrison looked over at Creed for some backup, the alpha of the Gray Backs wasn't even trying to hide his smile. "It's kind of funny."

"Yeah, except Audrey got hurt in this! She spent most of her savings getting here, and I didn't even know we were in a relationship!"

"She's pretty, isn't she?" Willa asked as she pulled her dyed red hair into a spiky pony-tail on top of her head.

"Doesn't matter what she looks like. I'm not ready for a mate, and I'm especially not ready to commit to a complete stranger."

"Oh, come on, Harrison. I screened her for you. I sifted through all the desperate humans looking to bang a Boarlander. You should be thanking me."

"Thanking you? Are you serious right now? You sent me a human. Me. The alpha of the most fucked-up crew of shifters, and you think a meek human woman is a good fit?"

"Ooooh, you silly, naïve, simple, little newborn baby. Go type her name into the shifter registration site. Your mate is no human."

Harrison stared at Willa, waiting for the punchline. When Willa got bored and sniffed her armpit, he took the bait. "What do you mean?"

"I mean, I went and found you a mate who can deal with Clinton, Bash, and your scary-ass bear, too. Have you read these?" she asked, yanking the papers from Creed's hand and holding them up. "You should. She's one of the good ones, Harrison."

"Why did you lure her up here, Willa?"

Willa grinned and walked away. Over her shoulder, she called out, "To get you living again. You're welcome. Almost Alpha, out." Remorselessly, she flicked her wrist in a tiny wave over her shoulder and made her way back to her mate, Matt, where she sank into his lap and rubbed his fake baby belly affectionately.

Creed grinned after her, then looked at Harrison. "Congratulations, man."

"Shut up," he grumbled as he made his way

back to his truck.

Beaston stood leaned against the driver's side door, head cocked, green eyes blazing. "I heard what Willa did. She's good. You should go see your mate before she leaves you." Beaston pushed off Harrison's truck and crossed his arms over his chest. "Audrey makes sense now."

Harrison had never liked giving Beaston his back, so he side-stepped to his truck and settled behind the wheel. As Harrison drove away, he looked to his rearview mirror once to see Beaston watching him leave with a strange smile crooking his lips.

Gripping the wheel, Harrison blasted away from Grayland Mobile Park, feeling even more unsettled than when he'd arrived.

FIVE

Audrey pulled her neatly folded shirts from the middle drawer of the dresser in her hotel room, then packed it in the corner of her suitcase. She regretted everything. Sure, she'd heard about people being tricked in online relationships, but she'd been careful and thought she'd asked all the right questions. She'd even called Clinton's phone once just to make sure the profiles were legit. It had gone to his voicemail, but it was definitely his number.

Her phone dinged from the bedside table where it was charging. It was the custom sound that said she had a message on her Bangaboarlander profile. Audrey sank down onto the stiff mattress and checked the message.

I had Bash hack the website and now the person who tricked you has no access. I'm sorry.
-H.

She bit her thumbnail and stared at the glowing screen. She waited a few minutes, debating an answer. Her heart could not take getting deceived again.

How do I know it's really Harrison this time and not some scammy life-ruiner?

She hit send and waited. A minute drifted by and then her phone dinged again.

You told me the other day that the kiss I gave you was the best you'd had. I feel the same. And it's probably a really bad idea that I just told you that because again, you really shouldn't want anything to do with a man like me.
-The Real H.

She read the first two sentences over and over, unable to believe Harrison was being so frank with her. He certainly didn't sound like whoever had impersonated him before. Heart pounding in her chest, she pulled the charger cord out of the phone and lay on the bed as she typed a response.

I'm about to leave. I'm packing right now.

Five minutes passed so she went back to stuffing her folded clothes into her suitcase distractedly, eyes coasting time and time again to the silent phone nestled on the pillow.

A knock sounded at the door. Maybe it was housekeeping. They hadn't been by yet today. She pulled open the door and there stood Harrison, even taller, wider, and more intimidating than she remembered.

"H-hello," she said.

His eyes tightened slightly at the corners as he looked her over. "I've been sitting in the parking lot for an hour trying to talk myself out of knocking. This is a bad idea."

"Uh, okay," she said, looking around at her small hotel room. "Do you want to come in?"

Harrison strode past and rounded on her as soon as she closed the door. "I know what you are. I mean I could guess now that I smell you. You aren't wearing that migraine-inducing perfume to mask your fur anymore. But...I mean I looked you up."

Her heart sank to her toes and, feeling

unstable, she sat on the chair by the two-seater table. "That's bad news."

"What? Why?"

"I don't like people knowing about that part of my life."

Harrison sat on the very edge of the bed and clasped his hands in front of him. "Explain."

"That's the point, Harrison. I don't want to explain to anyone."

"You don't like being a shifter." It was a statement, not a question, as if he already knew the answer.

"It's not that I don't like it. I just don't understand anything about myself. I grew up with a human dad. The animal came from my mom, but I never knew her."

"You haven't met other shifters?"

"Not until Shifter Night, which is the actual reason I was on Bangaboarlander.com. It wasn't for some shifter booty call. My dad just wanted me to find someone like myself so I don't feel so…I don't know…ashamed."

"Ashamed." Harrison rolled backward and locked his arms on the bed, then let off a single laugh. "Ashamed?" he repeated. "Woman, you're a fucking *tiger* shifter. There's no room for shame. Only badassery."

"Yeah, you know, that's what everyone thinks, but that's not the way it is. I have no control over my Changes, and I know nothing about shifter rules or appropriate behavior except what I've read on Cora Keller's website. That's pathetic, Harrison. All I've learned about *myself* is from the internet. It wasn't exactly my choice to come out and register."

Harrison's brows lowered. "Why did you then?"

"I was forced. God, this is so embarrassing," she muttered, her cheeks blazing. "I had an uncontrolled Change in my Jeep during rush-hour traffic on the way into the city. Those marks on the back seats? I did that, trying to escape my damned ride. In standstill traffic. The police had to tranquilize me. And now there's all these awful pictures on the internet of me lying on the pavement, all glossy-eyed with a dart sticking out of my shoulder."

Harrison snorted, but then coughed to cover it up.

"It's not funny. I was traumatized. Still am."

"Clearly, because you came seeking safety with the *Boarlanders*."

An accidental smile cracked her lips, but

she pursed them together to hide it. "This really isn't funny. I'm super messed up."

"Disagree. Clinton is messed up. Bash is messed up. I'm messed up. Hell, the entirety of the Gray Back Crew is messed up. From where I'm sitting, you're the most normal shifter I've met."

"Mmm," she murmured. "You haven't seen my animal. She's a bloodletting, rip-roaring, claws-out, bitey she-demon." A long snarl rattled her throat and tapered off to nothing as her animal disagreed. The heat in her cheeks spread to the tips of her ears.

"She sounds sexy as hell."

"Flatterer."

"No really, look." He pointed to his crotch. "That's a bona fide boner, tiger edition."

Sure enough, his long, thick shaft was bulging against the zipper of his jeans.

"My growl gave you an erection?"

"I like the growl, yes, but I like the way you smell without that perfume shit you wore the other day. I can smell your fur and your..."

"My what?"

He inhaled deeply and twitched a glance at her lap, then stared at the toe of his boot. "Forget it. Did you bring a bathing suit?"

"Yeah," she drawled out suspiciously.

"Good, go put it on. I'm taking you to the hot spring. You can't leave Saratoga without hitting all the tourist highlights."

"Really?"

"Yes, really. I'll be your tour guide. For today, at least. Tomorrow I have work to do."

"Cutting trees?" she asked as she dug through her suitcase for the black and white striped swimsuit she'd brought.

"Yeah, we'll do a shift tomorrow, but we're down half the crew. I have a couple of newcomers moving in tomorrow evening, and I need to help them settle."

"So they'll be Boarlanders?"

"Kind of. Kirk is a silverback shifter who works at the sawmill under Kong. Do you know him?"

"Well, I saw them at the bar the other night and I've heard of them. Or rather, read about them. I researched the shifters in Damon's mountains before I came here."

"Like some kind of detective?"

She giggled and shook her head. "I'm a waitress at a tiny diner in Buffalo Gap. I was just really excited and nervous about coming up here and finally meeting you, and I'm horrible with names, so I studied the crew pages on Cora Keller's website. Kong and Kirk registered officially around the same time I did last year."

Harrison was staring at her lips as she talked, and she grew self-conscious under his scrutiny, so she dipped her gaze to hide her flushing cheeks.

"So Kirk will be under me, but not as an official Boarlander. And I'm leeching Mason off the Gray Backs to help as well. He never pledged under Creed. He's there because his best friend, Damon, settled into Grayland Mobile Park with his mate, Clara, after their house was burned down by a"—Harrison cleared his throat and finished in a murmur—"rival dragon."

Audrey gave him one slow blink as she tried to absorb all that information. She was beginning to realize Cora's website was just scratching the surface. "Is Mason a shifter? I didn't see him on the website."

"And you won't if he can help it. You know how it is. When we register, we have to update where we live. Mason cut himself off from his people and likes living here without them coming after him."

"What is he? Wait, don't tell me. That's rude to ask, right?"

Harrison grinned such an easy smile, his

dark blue eyes danced with the expression. God, he was stunning. "It's considered rude to come out and ask someone what kind of animal they are, but it's different in Damon's mountains. Everyone knows everyone, and nobody gives a shit about etiquette. Not the Ashe Crew, not the Gray Backs, and certainly not my crew. Mason is a boar shifter. Not like one of those domestic pigs that lays around in the mud and eats slops, but a muscle-bound, razorback feral hog five times the size of the biggest one you'll see in the wild with long, curving tusks, eyes like a demon, and pitch black fur. He's a beast, but more importantly, he's a really hard worker and a good guy. I need him bad, and I owe Creed for letting me have him for the rest of the logging season. We're still short on labor, but with these guys, at least we have a shot at hitting Damon's numbers." Harrison frowned suddenly. "I can't believe I just told you all that."

"I won't tell anyone. I'm from a tiny town, and I was the only shifter there. I hid what I was for the first twenty-five years of my life. Your secrets are safe with me." Audrey held up her bathing suit. "I'm going to get dressed. I'll be right back."

Thank God she'd already shaved this

morning because she was excited about seeing the famous hot springs and spending time with Harrison. *The* Harrison, not the made up imposter who had tricked her into coming here.

In front of the mirror, she pulled her straight brunette locks into a high ponytail, slathered on another layer of lip gloss, then glared thoughtfully at the bottle of perfume sitting next to the sink. That had been her crutch. She'd used it for years, paranoid that other humans would somehow smell her fur and deem her "other." But here, she didn't have to wear that horrid scent-mask. There were shifters all over these mountains, and the people of Saratoga were used to them. Accepting even. It wasn't like Buffalo Gap where the town had revolted with the news that one of their own was a tiger shifter.

Plus, Harrison liked the way she smelled.

Audrey picked up the cold, half-full bottle and set it gently in the trashcan so the glass wouldn't break. And when she stood back up and looked at her reflection, she was proud of herself. Straightening her spine, she pulled on her swimsuit cover-up, opened the bathroom door, and walked out, a ready smile for Harrison on her face.

But when she saw what was settled in his lap, she lurched to a stop and gasped.

He turned the page and looked up at her with a slight frown marring his face. Uncertainty had pooled in his stormy eyes. He asked, "So, is this some kind of book about your life?"

Rushing forward, she closed the book and pulled it to her chest like armor. "It's stupid."

"It's really not," he argued, locking his arms against the mattress until his triceps bulged.

"It's a scrapbook."

"Do you make a lot of them?"

"No, just this one. I brought it in case I wanted to add a page after I met you."

"Let me see it."

"No. It's private. No one has seen it, and I like it that way."

"Why?"

Audrey gritted her teeth and looked away. No answer was best.

"Let me guess. You don't want me to see it because that's the real you in there. That's the little pieces you have kept hidden from everyone. Right?"

"You don't understand."

"I understand more than you think," he

said darkly. "I grew up an outsider, too. I had secrets to hide from everyone around me. It's lonely."

Tears burned her eyes, and she blinked them back. He did understand more than she'd assumed then, but she wasn't ready to expose herself so deeply with only a moment's notice.

"Audrey, I printed out every conversation you had on that matchmaking website. I wanted to read it so I could get to know you better, but three pages in, I was so pissed off I couldn't read any more."

Audrey hugged her scrapbook closer. "Why were you angry?"

Harrison's eyes had lightened to a frosty color, and a muscle near his mouth twitched. "Because it's not how this should've happened. It's not how I want to get to know you. I want you to tell me all that stuff, and reading the conversation between you and someone else felt like stealing. I don't want to steal that stuff, Audrey. I want you to give it to me."

"Well, I thought I did," she whispered. "I thought that *was* you, and you were falling in love with me, too…but I was alone in that."

Harrison searched her eyes, then leaned forward and held out his hand. "Then let me catch up."

Oh, she knew what he was asking for. He was asking for this huge piece of her that no one else knew about. He was asking for a part of her heart she'd kept only for herself. He was asking her to ignore the betrayal she'd endured and openly trust him.

Harrison Lang was the most dangerous man she'd ever met.

Audrey stared at the dingy, white, closed blinds of the single window and considered asking him to leave. She could tell him she wasn't into him, she couldn't do this anymore, or she'd simply been too hurt by the website betrayal.

But when she looked back at him, his eyes were steady, his palm still out, waiting, as if he really wanted to see this part of her. And if she didn't do this now, she might never let anyone in.

"Please don't laugh."

"I won't. I saw the first three pages, and they were really good. Sit by me and explain them."

Reluctantly, she handed him the heavy scrapbook and sank onto the bed next to him.

The front cover had cutout letters of her name on a blue background and a white housecat with black stripes she'd glued to the tame-looking critter.

Harrison pointed to it with his eyebrows arched up in question.

"The scrapbooking supply store didn't have tigers so I had to make one."

"Please fucking tell me you're a white tiger."

Her face cracked in a grin, and she closed her eyes to stifle the giddy sound in her throat. No one in her life had ever sounded hopeful about such things. "Yes," she admitted in a whisper.

"Daaaaaamn. Woman, do you know how rare you are?"

"Well, yes, because I tried to track down a mate who was a tiger like me because I thought that was what I was supposed to do. I didn't know at the time if hooking up with a human was…you know."

"Was what?"

"Taboo or gross."

"It's not. Shifters and humans hook up all the time. Creed's mate, Gia, is totally human, and she gave him a little bear cub."

"I figured that part out when I got ahold of the only other registered tiger. He was awful. He was interested in one thing. He was obsessed with talking about when I would go into heat."

"Why?"

Audrey pressed her cool palms against the fire in her cheeks and said low, "Because I become crazy for sex, or mating, or whatever you call it. I guess it's a big cat shifter thing. Anyway, I stopped talking to him when he turned raunchy."

"Okay, you and I are going to talk more about your heat when you aren't the color of a cherry Popsicle. Page one." He flipped past the cover page to the first spread.

It was a series of pictures of her when she was born. Her dad hugged her close in one snapshot, and in another, her mother held her. Audrey was tiny and red cheeked, crying, and her mom's head was angled down. All she could tell from this picture was that her mom had the same hair color as her. Her birthday was at the bottom in bubble letters.

Audrey pointed to the picture on the right. "That right there is the only picture I have of my mom."

Harrison jerked his gaze to her. "Seriously? You can't even see her face."

"She didn't like pictures. Dad said it was because she was like me, a tiger, and she liked to stay hidden. He snuck this one and gave it to me when I was seven and wouldn't quit asking about her."

"Why did she leave?"

"I think that some people are meant to be parents, and some are not. She had trouble staying in one place. Trouble staying sober. My dad said he was afraid to leave me alone with her when I was a baby, and when she left, it broke his heart, but he knew it was probably best for me. He wanted me to have stability, and she wasn't capable of giving it."

"Yeah, but your entire shifter heritage left with your mom."

Audrey shrugged helplessly. "That was the bad part, but the good part was that my dad knew exactly what I was from day one, and he moved us out to Buffalo Gap, bought some land, and raised me as well as he could. He kept everything as normal as possible. I went to school with other kids and had a parent who was completely devoted to being mom and dad. I had a good childhood. It was just missing her."

Harrison turned the page. There was a picture of her at Kindergarten graduation with a big, gap-toothed grin and pigtails. "You have freckles," he murmured, gripping the book.

"Yeah, under my make-up, I'm freckled.

Polka dots and stripes," she said with a nervous laugh.

This spread was on a purple background with cartoon diplomas and graduation caps glued in the top left corner. A picture at the bottom showed her dressed in her tiny cap and gown, up on Dad's shoulders, arms wrapped around his face while he cheesed through his giant mustache at the camera.

"He's a good man," Harrison said.

"He's the best. He was the one who encouraged me to sign up on Bangaboarlander. Not to actually bang a Boarlander, but to hopefully meet people like me. He didn't like that I felt so alone."

Harrison sighed and wrapped his arm around her shoulders as she flipped to the next page. It was a picture taken at her eighth birthday party. Dad had invited her entire second-grade class out to their trailer and set up rope swings in the tree out front and a slip-n-slide on the lawn, and he'd done a big barbecue cookout for all the kids' parents so they could watch their kids playing. In the picture, all the kids were standing in front of her house with pointy party hats and grins and peace signs, while Audrey stood on the very outskirt, her lips barely lifted in a smile and her eyes looking hollow.

"You lived in a trailer?" Harrison asked, pointing to the old singlewide she'd grown up in. Dad lived there still.

"Yeah, it was the only way dad could afford the land for me to Change safely. It was hard for me to connect with other kids. I was always afraid they would figure out I was a monster, so it was hard keeping friends and fitting in."

"You look sad."

"I had fun, but I felt sick as all get-out. I hadn't Changed in a long time, and I fought my cat hard that entire party. I was so scared she would come out in front of everyone. I Changed on accident about an hour after everyone left. That was the last birthday party we did with my classmates. Too risky. I think my dad was just desperately trying to integrate me into my class and the town."

She flipped through more pages, explaining as she went. Some were of school events, cheerleader tryouts, a birthday card Mom sent her one year, a letter from her dad on the day of her high school graduation telling her how proud he was. Her diploma, a copy of her first paycheck from Donna's Diner, an employee-of-the-month award, a receipt with a nice note from a regular customer. There was a spread with pictures she hadn't known her dad had taken of her over the years. There was one a year since, from ages five to eighteen, swinging on the same tree swing. He gifted them to her for her twentieth birthday. "For the scrapbook," he'd declared. In each one, she'd grown, but one thing was always the same—her smile.

"You were happy there," Harrison said, pointing to the last picture of her, mid-laugh, hair flying behind her as she kicked her legs to go higher.

"Yeah. It was my little paradise. Dad made it a happy place."

"Happy but lonely."

Her voice would tremble if she said anything, so instead, she nodded and turned the page. This was the second to last spread of the book. It was green, her favorite color. She fingered the picture of January, her ex-boyfriend's three-year-old girl. "I was lonely until this page," she said, her eyes burning.

Harrison hugged her closer. "Who is this?"

"I started dating someone I'd grown up with. A human. His name was Rhett, and he shared custody of his kid. This is January. I loved her. Love her still. She felt like mine for the year Rhett and I were together."

Harrison fingered the piece of tape with a torn picture still attached. She'd ripped out of her book the photo of her and Rhett grinning for the camera the day he'd let her down. January still deserved to be in it, though.

"Why did you stop dating him?"

"It wasn't my choice." She flipped to the next page. Across the top was the date she'd Changed in the car and been outed as a tiger shifter. The rest of the spread was covered in layers of newspaper clippings, all about her, and all with that awful picture of her tranquilized and semiconscious on the pavement. "Less than a thousand people live there, so this was huge news. I was forced to register, and Rhett came over right after it happened and said he didn't want January around someone like me. He said it was wrong for us to be together, and he didn't want me anymore. He asked for his ring back." She swallowed hard and closed the book on Harrison's lap. "And that was that. The tiger took everything." A long snarl vibrated in her chest, but she didn't stifle it. Both she and her animal had been devastated in the aftermath.

Harrison set the book aside and wrapped her up in a hug, pulling her tight against his chest as he rocked them back and forth slowly. "The town would've gotten used to you eventually, Audrey. Humans aren't bad. They're just scared of what they don't understand."

"*You* don't understand. It's not the same out there in the world for people like us. If there is only one shifter, people don't get used to them. It only works if there are big groups and humans willing to accept them or move away. I saved all year to move to Breckenridge, Colorado because the Breck Crew have paved the way for a really accepting community. I thought I could be safe and happy there. Like people wouldn't stare at me, whisper, and shield their kids when I passed them on the street. I thought maybe if I was part of a pro-shifter community, I could feel normal. When you responded to my message on the matchmaking site, I thought it was a sign that my life was moving in a different direction. Maybe a better direction than I imagined."

"So you spent your savings to come here and meet me."

"Yeah. Pretty pathetic, huh?"

Harrison rested his cheek against her hair and murmured, "Hell no. It's brave. You wanted a different life, and you went after it. There's nothing pathetic about that, Audrey. What you've done is admirable."

He felt so good, so strong, holding her like this. Like everything hadn't gotten messed up. She inhaled his scent—shaving cream and crisp, masculine soap—and closed her eyes just to get lost in this moment. She might never get another like this, where she felt utterly safe.

Harrison eased back by inches, and his lips were so close. She could hear the hitch in his breathing as he froze there, hesitating. *Kiss me.*

He lifted his lightened gaze from her lips to her eyes, then closed the last bit of space between them. His mouth turned soft, kneading against her, drinking her in. Audrey gripped his T-shirt and parted her lips slightly. Harrison slipped his tongue inside and brushed against hers, just barely, then withdrew with a sexy smack. It had ended too soon, so she waited a moment too long to open her eyes.

Harrison was looking at her with the strangest expression. Confusion mixed with wonder.

"Did I do it wrong?"

He barked a laugh and pulled her hand

against his crotch. His boner was back and bigger than ever. "Woman, you did nothing wrong. I just don't want to push too hard too fast."

"Too hard, too fast," she repeated in a dreamy voice as she brushed her hand up the hard length of his dick.

Harrison let off a tiny moan and relaxed back on locked arms, pushing his hips up to meet her touch. "You're purring."

Startled, Audrey stifled the sound in her throat and jerked her hand away from him. "I'm not some housecat and technically, big cats don't purr," she rushed out. "We snarl, and sometimes it just sounds happier than other times." She winced at how lame she was being right now.

"That sounded like a purr to me." Harrison caught her fingertips and brushed his lips against them with a wicked smile. "I love that sound," he growled out, eyes locked on hers.

She relaxed and let off a soft, happy, vibrating noise, just for him, because she trusted him. Because he had seen her scrapbook, seen the parts of her life she kept hidden, and had somehow made her feel better...and stronger. He made her feel like a tigress instead of a kitten.

She would reward him for empowering her instead of putting her down.

Carefully, she knelt between his legs and popped the button of his jeans. Her fingers shook, and she winced. *Be the tiger.* When she looked up at him, his eyes were bright and hungry. Warmth pooled between her legs as he leaned back on one locked arm and brushed her hair from her face with the other.

The corner of his lips lifted in a sexy smile. "Are you going to go and change everything between us?"

"Do you want that?" she asked tentatively as she unzipped his jeans.

"I wanted to take this as slowly as you need." He let off a sigh and rocked his hips forward as she pulled his pants down, unsheathing his erection. "I wanted to do this right."

"This feels right to me," she whispered.

"One rule," he gritted out as she ran her fingertips up the length of his hard shaft. "Don't give me your back."

Frowning up at him, she asked, "What do you mean?"

"I mean, if you don't want a claiming mark from me, don't let me have your back. This feels different. It feels big with you." His voice was completely inhuman now. Rough and deep. She loved it.

She didn't know rules about claiming marks, as he called them, but she would ask him about that later. Right now, she would be careful not to give him her back, and enjoy this intimacy. She'd fallen twice for him—the first time in the messages on the website, and now, as she got to know the real man behind Harrison's stoic mask, she fell even deeper.

Another purr rattled her throat as she gripped him at his base and slid her lips over him. Harrison went rigid under her and let off another soft moan. His hand tightened in her hair, but he stayed gentle enough as he guided her deeper. His dick throbbed in her mouth, and she traced his head with her tongue, then released him slowly. Harrison positioned himself closer to the edge of the bed, tugged her cover-up over her head, and then pulled the hair band from her ponytail, releasing her tresses. With a sexy smile, he drew her closer and spread his legs wider for her as his hips rolled forward.

He wanted her to go faster, she could tell, but what fun would that be? He was twitching under her, growling, breath ragged already. She could have him in a minute if she let him lead, but then it would be over, and she wanted to play for their first time. She dragged her nails down the inside of his thighs and reveled in the gooseflesh she conjured with her touch.

She took him again, deeply, careful to keep her teeth off his skin. She couldn't stop purring if she wanted to. The head of his cock tasted salty, and she smiled. Harrison rocked against her every time she took him, and when she pushed his shirt up to expose his abs, they were flexing with his graceful movement. He was the sexiest man she'd ever seen, and he was here with her, moaning her name, flexing under her because she made him feel good.

Teasing him, she bit his inner thigh, then took him in her mouth again. Every muscle in his body was rigid now as he grunted out a helpless sound.

She could feel it. The hormone surge caused by whatever animal magnetism Harrison possessed was drawing her tiger out. She arched her back and pulled her lips off him.

"Fuck, woman, you smell so good," Harrison rasped out.

She could smell herself too—pheromones and arousal.

Audrey offered him a feline smile as she stood and shoved the suitcase off the bed. She crawled onto the mattress and broke his rule by getting on her hands and knees and presenting her back. She swayed backward, toward him, her bathing suit soaking between her thighs.

She watched him over her shoulder as she bowed her back and lifted her ass in the air. She wanted to claw the sheets and beg him to cover her. Everything was fuzzy and warm, and her blood buzzed like she'd had too much to drink. She was drunk on Harrison. This hadn't ever happened, but she was helpless to take it back. She was his.

She rocked back toward him again, pleading, the purr in her throat growing louder as his calloused hand gripped her waist. He'd shucked his pants and pulled his shirt off, and his eyes looked just as hazy with lust as she felt.

"Naughty little renegade, breaking my rules," he murmured, eyes on the bottom half of her swimsuit. He plucked at the tie on one side, then the other, then pulled the strip of fabric away from her and let it drop onto the floor.

His long, thick shaft jutted out from his

powerful body. She'd had to be gentle with Rhett, but she would never have that problem with Harrison. Scarred up, dominant alpha grizzly. She couldn't hurt him.

He shoved her knees wider with his own, then gripped her waist in both hands as he rocked forward and teased her wet entrance with the head of his cock.

"Ooooh," she moaned as she arched her spine and rocked backward, chasing him.

His lips were soft on her shoulder blade, and he whispered against her skin, "You want me in you?"

"Yes," she pleaded, rocking back again.

He flexed his abs and slid into her, slowly until he was fully immersed inside her. His fingers dug into her waist as he let off a low growl. He blew out a shaky breath as he eased out of her, then rammed back into her again.

She rested on her elbows to give him better access and clutched at the comforter. He was huge and stretched her, but the pleasure outweighed the burn. High on endorphins, she slid her hand between her legs and touched her clit. Harrison's hand slid over hers, pressing her own touch against herself as his teeth grazed her shoulder blade. He moved within her in a slow rhythm, but a few strokes more, and his control slipped. His body was tensing now as he rammed into her faster, and there was his gentle bite again, right against her shoulder blade. God, she loved this.

The pressure built between her legs, and now he was going so deep she could feel his balls hitting her hand. He bit down hard, but reared back just before he pierced her skin. He pulled her upward, and a dizzying moment later, she was off the bed and against the door. Rough, sexy bear. He slipped his hand into the top of her bathing suit and cupped her aching breast as he kissed her, tongue against hers in a desperate rhythm.

"Finish me," she whispered against his lips.

Harrison snarled and lifted her off the ground, then slid into her. His kiss was rough as he rammed into her hard and fast, and with a cry of ecstasy, Audrey threw her head back against the door, blinded by how good he felt inside of her.

Orgasm exploded through her, and she gripped his hair, closing her eyes to the world. Her body gripped him in throbbing pulses as she murmured his name. He bucked into her faster and gritted out a feral snarl as he went rigid against her. His dick swelled and throbbed, matching her own release as he shot warmth into her.

His movement slowed and turned graceful again. Oh, clever bear. He knew how to draw every aftershock from her body. Gently, he lowered her to her feet and cupped her neck. There was no teasing smile now as he trapped her in his bright blue gaze. Chest heaving, he lowered his lips to hers and kissed her softly. Relaxing against him, she gripped his wrists to keep his touch there and sucked on his bottom lip.

"Let me clean you," he whispered against her ear.

Surprised by how caring he was and at a loss for words, she nodded and kissed him one last time as he pulled out of her. Warmth trickled down her thighs. She swayed without the support of his strong arms, so she locked her legs and leaned her back against the door in an attempt to stay upright.

Before he turned away from her, he gave her a crooked, naughty smile. "You should've run while you had the chance, kitty."

"Mmm," she hummed, glowing under that nickname murmured in his deep, sexy timbre. "And why's that?"

Harrison lifted his chin and locked his

possessive gaze on her. "Because you're mine now."

SIX

"Okay, change of plans," Harrison said as he spiked up his hair in the mirror. "You drained me, woman, and now I'm starving."

Audrey giggled as she shoved a beach towel into her black, sparkly tote bag. "Me, too. I heard a rumor about how much bear shifters eat."

Harrison straightened his tight forest green T-shirt with a beer logo on the front onto his torso. "It's true. Whatever you heard, it's true."

Harrison opened the door and took the tote bag from her as she passed.

Pleased as punch, she smiled her thanks. "So you do like copious amounts of salads then?"

"Ha, no. I need meat."

"But not raw meat."

"Do you like raw meat?"

"Ew!" she exclaimed. "No. I was lonely growing up, but I never once got the craving for a friendly tapeworm."

Harrison snorted and opened the passenger's side door of a jacked-up red Chevy Silverado. She angled her face at the expensive looking black-out rims and matching step-ups. "This is a nice truck."

"You sound surprised."

"Well, your trailer park looks like a shithole."

He bellowed a single laugh and helped her into his pickup. "Yeah, well, that you can blame on Clinton. I've wanted to fix it up, and Damon gave us the funds to do it a long time ago, but Clinton is convinced if we repair anything in the trailer park, we're fixing it up so we can bring in girls and make it more accessible for cubs. You look sexy as fuck with your hair down." Harrison leaned over her and sipped her lips before he grinned and closed the door, then jogged around the front of his truck and got in behind the wheel.

Audrey wrapped her arms around her stomach to settle the butterflies there, but it didn't help. Harrison was wrecking her entire system, and now she would never stop smiling.

"Why doesn't Clinton like women?"

"That I don't know." Harrison rested a hand behind her headrest and checked the parking lot behind them as he backed out. "Clinton is a tough egg to crack."

"Will he be angry that we're...what are we?" *Please don't say fuck buddies.*

"Dating. Mating. Whatever you want to call us, I'm good with."

"Dating is good." *For now.* "I mean, technically we've been dating for a couple of months," she teased.

"Oh, that's right," he played along. "To celebrate our two month anniversary, I'm going to take you to the opening week of the first and only Thai food restaurant in town."

"Ooh, yum! Have you ever been there?"

"Never. It'll be a first for both of us."

"First date," she murmured, in disbelief that she was really riding through Saratoga with Harrison.

"And your first Boarlander bang. That was your fault, by the way. I was happy to just kiss you and go sit in some boiling hot spring so I could have the excuse of getting to know you. You went all dick-sucky on me, ya little vixen."

"Vixens are foxes. My claws are bigger."

"That they are." Harrison pulled to a stop at the red light and lifted the back of his shirt. Among his scars were long, healing scratches.

Her mouth flopped open as she traced one. "Did I do that?"

"Yeah, kitty." He pulled her pink painted nails to his lips and kissed her quick as the light turned green. Hitting the gas, he said, "You can mark me up with those sexy painted claws of yours anytime."

"Just so you know, I kind of lost my mind with you back there. I'm not like that."

"Like what?"

Easy. "Um, so you know how I told you about my ex, Rhett?"

"Yeah, talking about him makes me want to break things, so perhaps let's not." Indeed, Harrison's eyes were lightening by the moment, and the air had grown heavier in the cab of his truck. "It was crappy of him to bail on you when you were going through such a hard time. Pisses me off thinking about you going through that alone because he wasn't man enough to stick around."

Harrison was much more dominant than her animal, but she forced her hand on top of his tense thigh. "What I mean to say is, he's the only other man I've been with. So...you know…don't break my heart."

Harrison twitched his attention to her, then back to the road, then to her again. He smiled slow and intertwined his fingers with hers. "Same to you."

"Mmm hmm, except I follow you on social media, and I see all the shifter groupies you bang. They tag you in their posts."

"What? I set that up two years ago, and I never post on it. I don't even check it."

"Well, every girl you sleep with seems happy to brag about it and post pictures with you."

He gave her a disbelieving look and shook his head. "Three."

"Three what?"

"I've slept with three women, and two of those were relationships. Short-lived and years ago, but they still counted as girlfriends. The last one…well, she was a mistake. I went home with a groupie. I was lonely…" He made a single clicking sound behind his teeth. "It doesn't matter. Do you know how many pictures I take with women? Ten on any given night at Sammy's. That's part of the gig. The Boarlanders are still single, and Jake, the owner of the bar, takes care of us if we flirt a little and play the game. Anyone posting pictures saying I slept with them is full of shit and looking for attention."

"Oh." Well that was different from what she'd thought.

"Listen to my voice. You'll be able to tell if someone is being dishonest if you really *hear* them. They'll sound off, false, if they are lying. Shifter lesson for the day," he said with a wink.

Huh. She'd suspected she could kind of tell, but hadn't been one hundred percent sure. She would have to practice lie detection. Audrey straightened the hem of her black cotton cover-up, which today, doubled as a dress that rested halfway up her thighs. "Four." She gave him a half smile because that's all she could muster when talking about women he'd been with. She wanted to claw every one of their faces off. "I'm number four."

"Wrong, kitty. You aren't a number, and I don't ever want you sayin' it like that again." He squeezed her hand. "You're different."

The fast food Thai place was hopping, but considering the small size of the town, this very well might've been the event of the season. Audrey thought Harrison might be more withdrawn out in public because of his reputation with the town and his crew and all, but after parking, he stood in line with her and didn't withhold an ounce of affection. He brushed her back and rubbed little circles between her shoulder blades. He held her hand, and twice he leaned over and kissed her on the temple.

"You're a teddy bear," she accused.

"Ha!" Harrison laughed as he held the glass door open and let her pass under his arm. "No one has ever accused me of that before. Distant, quiet, moody, sure." The smile dipped from his lips as he stared thoughtfully at her. "I don't know what it is, but you're easy to be around. You make me..." Harrison lifted his shoulder in a shrug. "You know."

Her cheeks were flushing with heat again, but not from embarrassment this time. "Say it," she said, poking him in the ribs.

Harrison lifted her hand and bit her wrist gently, then shook his head and looked up at the giant menu behind the counter.

"Distant, quiet, moody," she repeated.

"Stop. It's just different with you. Easier. I don't have to hide, or be gentle, and you've gone through something hard. So did I. It feels nice not to feel like the only one." He cast her a quick glance and then muttered too low for any of the surrounding humans to hear, "You make me happy."

"I knew it." She clapped once and tried and failed to contain her gloating smile. "I *knew* it!"

"Okay, all right, what do you want to eat?" he muttered.

"Red Curry, and I want it spicy. Like, level three spicy. And crab rolls. And soup," she mumbled scouring the menu. "I'm hungry."

When she looked up at Harrison, he was grinning at her like she was the cutest thing he'd ever seen. Audrey bumped his shoulder and bathed in how happy she was when his warmth seeped through the sleeve of her cover-up. Her black glittery flip-flops clacked as they approached the counter, and after Harrison ordered their food, they made their way to one of the tables on the back patio. It was warm and pretty outside, and the umbrella over the table blocked the direct sunlight. Harrison sat across from her and squeezed his ankles around hers as he dug in.

"I needed today," he said between bites. "I've been going so long where I didn't have a good day, and this feels like a recharge."

"Is it hard being an alpha?"

He inhaled deeply and took a long drink of his ice water. "It shouldn't be this hard. I used to be good at this, but lately it feels like I let my entire crew down. I'm not hitting the numbers Damon wants, and because of that, we're slowing down the new jobsites. Half of my crew left, and the ones I have left are at each other's throats. And you were right when you said our trailer park looks like a shithole."

"But you're strong. You'll fix your crew."

He smiled but his eyes still stayed hollow. "I don't care how strong you are. If you go through the suck long enough, it'll take its toll. It's been nice spending a day away from the drama at the park."

Audrey gulped a spoonful of soup. "What does Missionary Impossible mean?"

Harrison dropped his head and chuckled. "Bash wrote that on the sign when I turned down his request to let women in the park for the tenth time. Missionary position? He was pissed at me and Clinton, so he spray-painted the sign out of revenge. I'm gonna make his ass climb back up there and scrub it off."

"You should. And you should lift the 'no girls allowed' rule because I want to visit your park again." She grinned brightly and shoveled another bite of soup into her maw.

"Oh yeah?" His eyes narrowed. He rested his elbows on the table and clasped his hands in front of his mouth. "What else do you think I should do?"

"Call Clinton out on his shit, fix up your park however you want to, move those new shifters in, and start hitting those numbers like the badass Boss Bear you are. I mean, look at you. You're built like a freaking freight train, are covered in scars that somehow didn't kill you, and plus, on the internet, I saw a picture of you fighting Kong at some backwoods brawl house. I saw you go to battle with Clinton the other day. It was thirty seconds of beast mode, and then he was limp on the ground. And his bear is *huge*. You could fix anything."

"Get all that stuff done and dig my crew out of this massive hole, just like that."

"Just like that. Try this. It's amazing." She shoved the last half of her soup toward him, and then stole a scoop of crab fried rice from his plate. He'd ordered his in kill-me spicy though, so all she tasted was fire and pain.

Harrison laughed as she gulped down half her water to extinguish the flames on her tongue. He cocked his head and squeezed her ankles with his under the table. "You've been through a lot, but you're still optimistic."

"Everyone's been through a lot, Harrison. Life is hard, and sometimes it sucks, but you were the one who told me it was admirable that I saw a life I wanted and went after it."

She tucked a flyaway lock of hair behind her ear and softened her voice. "Go after the life *you* want."

SEVEN

Audrey dipped her toe in the hot spring and grinned. The evening shadows stretched across the stone surface surrounding the pool, and the air had cooled considerably. This had been the best day of her life, by a lot. After lunch, she'd spent the entire afternoon window shopping with Harrison. It had been an incredible opportunity to get to know him better, and the more she learned, the harder she was falling for the alpha of the Boarlanders.

He'd changed into a pair of navy blue swim trunks that hung just right on his tapered waist, and as he peeled off his shirt, she was stunned once again that he was hers. Or at least, he felt like hers. And from the purr in her throat, her inner tiger agreed.

Audrey kicked off her flip-flops and pulled

her cover-up over her head, only a little self-conscious when Harrison dragged his gaze down her body and back up. His "Damn, woman" had her nerves settled right down, though.

She couldn't explain it, but she was more confident around Harrison. More open, and it was easier to be outgoing. Outside of the restaurant, a trio of kids had asked to take a picture with him, and he'd told them Audrey was a white tiger shifter. Though she'd been mortified about him outing her, the kids had asked to take a picture with her, too. And afterward, they'd asked her to sign an autograph, right under Harrison's signature on a piece of paper. How cool was that? No one in Buffalo Gap had ever asked her for her signature unless she was signing for a speeding ticket.

The hobo hot spring looked like a pool with a bath house and everything, but the water was from a natural spring that filtered into it. Steam rose from the surface, and just as she was about to make her way down the steps, Harrison wrapped an arm around her and hooked a finger under her chin. He kissed her until her legs went numb and then smiled against her lips. "I like you."

"I like you two months more," she countered.

With a playful growl, Harrison picked her up and carried her over his shoulder into the pool, and she gasped at how shockingly warm it was. It was close to sunset, and they had the hot spring to themselves, so she slid her arms around Harrison's neck and wrapped her legs around him as he turned them in lazy circles.

"You read my scrapbook," she said.

"I sure did. And I'll read it again when you make a page dedicated to Saratoga."

"Now it's your turn. Share your scrapbook with me."

"Booo," he murmured. "Let's keep having fun instead."

With a happy sigh, she laid back into the floating position. "Tell me all your secrets, Boss Bear."

"Fine," he grumbled, placing his hands under her back and spinning her slowly. "When I was five, I lost my first tooth at baseball practice, and when I was eight, I stole a pack of tootsie rolls from the grocery store and had to return them *and* apologize, and when I was nine—"

"Harrison."

"I didn't have a mom, either."

Well, that drew her up short. "What happened to her?" Audrey asked cautiously.

Harrison twitched his head and stared at the sunrise, and for a while, the only sound was the gently lapping water against her body. "She's buried in a cemetery where I grew up in Montana. I used to go visit her all the time. I couldn't really remember what she looked like without studying a picture, but I remember how she used to hug me up tight before bed. I slept best when she was squeezing me. Safe," he murmured. "My dad was an asshole who liked to beat on us both, but my mom somehow made my room feel like he couldn't hurt us there."

"Oh, my God," she whispered, sitting up in the water. She shouldn't have done this. She shouldn't have dragged demons like this to the surface. She was hurting him. That much was apparent in his voice. "I'm sorry, Harrison."

"It happened a long time ago. Doesn't matter now."

She hugged him tightly and rested her chin on his shoulder as the sunset lit up the evening sky with vibrant oranges and pinks.

Harrison swallowed audibly and kissed her neck. "She died when I was seven, and then my room wasn't safe anymore. My dad was a drinker and easily offended. I couldn't walk carefully enough on the eggshells that made up the floor of that house. So here I am, a full-grown, mature male, my dad is out of my life, and I still can't have a good night. I know it sounds crazy, but letting my body go vulnerable is a battle every time I try and go to sleep. I have to patrol the border of Boarlander property to make sure not only that I'm safe, but my crew is safe, too. It's a compulsive thing. I can't sleep or settle if I don't. I almost got a grip on it a couple years ago, but shifter poachers hunted my crew, and I cut them off at the border of my territory."

Audrey's heart was breaking for him. Slowly, she eased back enough to trace the bullet scars on his torso. "Is that where you got these?"

Harrison huffed a humorless sound, and his eyes looked dark, so sad. "One of the Gray Backs, Georgia, tried to save me. She was human at the time and got riddled with their fire, just because she wanted me to live so bad. She was lying there on the ground, painting the forest floor red, and I just wanted to reach her so she didn't have to die alone."

"Did she live?"

"Barely. Jason, her mate, Turned her to

save her."

"And what happened to you?"

"The bears went to battle. Ashe Crew. Gray Backs. My boys. Damon was raining dragon's fire all around us, and one of my Boarlanders went to work trying to get the led out of my body. It took me a month to recover. That's a helluva lot of time for a shifter to heal. And while I was down, there was chaos in my crew. When a dominant animal is hurt, it riles up the others, makes them want to take over. So I was fighting, trying to hold alpha, and everyone was pissed. No one felt safe after that attack, and the hierarchy in my crew went to shit. I blame Clinton for pushing them out, but we were broken before he came along. He just deepened the cracks in my crew because he's spiraling. We would've been okay if we'd been whole to begin with."

"That's not on you, Harrison."

"It kind of is. As an alpha, it's my job to shoulder the responsibility. I was always dominant and a brawler. My dad made me that way, but having a crew under you is more than just fighting. You have to balance your people's needs, and somewhere along the way, that got all fucked up. It's not all my fault, but it's my responsibility to repair those cracks as we go, and I let too many get away from me." He frowned. "And again, I don't know why I'm telling you all this."

"Because I'm a witch and I drugged your ice water with truth serum."

Relief unfurled inside her when Harrison cracked a slight smile. He hugged her waist closer and dragged her body up against his erection. "You have bewitched me," he murmured just before he kissed her.

The rumbling sound of car engines sounded in the distance, prickling at Audrey's sensitive ears. Several trucks came to a stop in the parking lot outside the fence, their headlights making her squint and ease out of the lip-lock.

"Stop banging the Boarlander," a woman called. "We're coming in and I have delicate, virgin eyeballs."

"Aw crap," Harrison muttered, shaking his head. "I apologize for everything that is said from this moment on."

A small herd of people were filing out of the different-sized pickup trucks, and the sound of clacking flip-flops and the rolling wheels of a cooler echoed through the night.

"Who are they?" she asked, gripping Harrison tighter.

"You are about to meet some more of the shifters of Damon's mountains."

"Ah," she exclaimed as she pushed off Harrison like she'd been caught at a junior high make-out party.

"No," he murmured, gripping her waist. "It's okay. Most of them are paired up, too."

"Yoo-hoo," a tiny red-headed woman who led the way through the bath house doors called. She wore an oversize tote bag and a pair of horn-rimmed glasses on top of her head like a headband. She carried what looked like a giant canvas as the others filed in behind her, talking and cutting up.

"Audrey Foster, I'm Willa, also known as Almost Alpha of the Gray Backs, or Willa Wonka, or Nerd. This beefcake is not my man servant," she said pointing to a huge, shirtless, scarred-up, sandy-haired bruin beside her. "He is my mate, Matt, also known as Griz."

Matt waved and grinned. "I've heard a lot about you."

"You have?" Audrey asked. "From who?"

"From Willa. She kind of dated you."

"I'm super confused," Audrey murmured as she watched the group peel out of their shoes and pass around beers from the cooler.

"I might have accidentally set up a website

and flirted with you a lot, then invited you up here to meet Harrison."

Audrey gasped as red hot fury blasted through her. "That was you? Why did you do that?" Her voice had gone shrill, but frick it all, she was pissed.

"So you could meet the man of your dreams, and he could meet you," Willa said in a voice that said it should've been obvious. "I've brought you presents to buy your love and apologize. First…" Willa flipped around the canvas in her hands. "I took a painting class from the first lady of the Ashe Crew, Mrs. Brooke James herself, and I made this just for you."

The painting was of a terrible, uneven rainbow in a blue sky with a tiger and a bear holding hands in a meadow of eye-scorching neon flowers and worms. One of the bear's eyes was much bigger than the other, and the tiger was skipping on legs that were way too short.

"That looks like a first grader painted it," Harrison muttered.

"Thank you. Next, I have brought you a fine batch of worms." Willa handed the painting to Matt, and he traded her for a cardboard container with a lid on it. She flipped her hand around in circles, then bowed. She plucked the lid off, exposing a mass of slimy earthworms writhing around in a lump of black dirt. "You may use them for fishing, but they make better pets." She pointed to each of the worms in turn. "This one is Norma Dean Wiggles-Too-Much, there's Beatrice the Great, Handsy Thomas, Chuck the Perv, Princess Butter-Nipples, and Steven."

"Thank you?" Audrey said, trying not to scrunch up her face in disgust.

"And lastly, a fruity beer, because when we were online dating, I remember you told me that was your favorite." Willa handed her a purple pomegranate brewsky and grinned brightly. "And now for my apology. Prepare thyself." She inhaled deeply, then murmured, "You're welcome for my matchmaking services."

"That was literally the worst apology in the universe," Harrison said.

"That's ridiculous. Have you heard every apology in the universe?"

Audrey took the beer from Willa's hand and said, "I guess since it turned out okay, I forgive you."

"Great." Willa waved gallantly to the people slipping into the hot springs. "These are the Gray Backs. Or most of them. Damon and Clara are at home because she just pooped out a baby, and they're on babysitting duty for Creed's rug rat. Mason isn't here because he's packing to move to one of the lovely shit-shacks in Harrison's trailer park tomorrow. That's Creed," she said pointing to the dark-haired giant closest to them. "Gia, Georgia, Jason, Aviana," she said, pointing to the pregnant woman who had saved Audrey from standing in the long line at Sammy's. "And that scary beary back there," Willa said, pointing to the wild man with the glowing eyes who limped along the edge of the hot spring, "is Beaston. Don't get too close to him. He bites." Willa waggled her eyebrows.

"You shouldn't tell her that. I don't bite."

"You Changed me, didn't you?"

"One time, and you broke my leg."

"Beaston," Jason said, hugging Georgia at the edge of the water, "it doesn't make sense when you say you Changed her one time. It only takes one bite."

"Anyway, I believe you met Bash and Clinton. I can tell because Clinton was reciting love poems about you the entire drive here."

"I was bitching about her," Clinton said grumpily from the chair he'd plopped into beside the spring.

Bash jumped in, cannon-ball-style, splashing them all, and when he came up for air, he had a big goofy grin on his face. He shook his head like a dog and said, "I like Audrey."

Harrison growled when Bash swam too close, and Audrey stifled the giggles that were ready to bubble up her throat.

Beaston sat on the edge beside Aviana, dipping his feet in, his hand on the swell of his mate's stomach. "Audrey is going to bleed you, Clinton," he said blandly.

Willa snickered and eased herself over the edge and into Matt's arms. "When you do, invite me. I'll bring turkey jerky and green M&Ms. That bunion made the entire drive here miserable."

"Well, Audrey's presence here makes me miserable, but no one seems to care—"

"Shut up, Clinton," the Gray Backs, Bash, and Harrison all said at once.

Audrey took a deep drink of her fruity beer to keep her laughter inside as everyone went back to talking.

The night wore on, and the air was filled with constant chatter and laughter. One by one, the Gray Backs talked to her and shook her hand. She was three beers deep before she felt overheated and sat on the edge of the pool with Aviana and Beaston. Harrison settled between her legs, shootin' the shit with Creed and Georgia, and every once in a while he would turn his face and kiss the inside of her knee and go back to talking without missing a beat, as if he didn't realize he was giving her the affection.

Eventually, Georgia climbed up on Jason's back and chicken-fought Willa and Matt, which was hilarious, because those bear shifters under the women weren't going down for anything. It was twenty minutes before they called it a draw and swore to never play again.

"Look," Aviana whispered, pointing to her belly. She wore a black bikini, and her round belly was rolling strangely.

"The baby is moving?" Audrey whispered in awe.

"Yeah, you want to feel him?"

Audrey locked eyes on Aviana's to make sure she wasn't teasing, but she looked serious enough, and Beaston moved his hand to the other side of her belly to make room for Audrey's palm. With a nod, she touched right over where the baby rolled languidly. How incredible to feel life so new.

"He'll be a raven," Aviana murmured, dragging Audrey's hand to chase the movement.

"How do you know?"

"My mate dreamed it, and he's never wrong." Aviana cocked her head in a very bird-like fashion and pitched her voice low. "You *will* bleed Clinton."

Audrey jerked her gaze to where Clinton sat on a lounge chair, his eyes glowing eerily in the single porch light of the bathhouse. He was staring at her, as if he'd heard Aviana's prediction.

"That's not what I want," Audrey said.

"Don't want to, but need to," Beaston murmured low. "Change needs to happen. For you, but also for him." Beason twitched his chin at Harrison, who was laughing at something Matt said.

Fixing anything with bloodletting was the most barbaric thing she'd ever heard, and goose bumps lifted over her body as she pulled her hand off Aviana's belly. The next time she looked up, Clinton wasn't sitting in the lounge chair anymore. He was making his way through the parking lot toward Harrison's truck with long, deliberate strides, as if he couldn't get away from her fast enough.

A vision of her sitting beneath the Boarland Mobile Park sign in the form of her white tiger flashed across her mind like lightning. From where she sat, a long, steaming fissure broke the earth and created a yawning chasm between Harrison and Bash on one side and Clinton on the other.

She could suddenly see them—the spider web of cracks Harrison had talked about in the Boarlander Crew.

For reasons she couldn't understand, Audrey suddenly got the feeling she would be the biggest one of all.

EIGHT

Harrison ripped the cord of the chainsaw and lowered his sunglasses over his eyes. Settling the blade into the dead bark of the beetle-infested tree, he cut out a wedge and stepped nimbly out of the way when the wind pushed it close to him as it fell.

"Number!" Bash called from sixty yards away where he'd just felled a tree of his own.

"Thirty more," Harrison said, wiping the number out of his head so he could start over.

Bash was an anomaly. He was a simple man with simple desires, but he was borderline genius with numbers. He didn't keep notes. He just remembered every calculation at the end of each shift. It was he who had invested their money and built their retirement accounts. Harrison didn't talk about that stuff with people. Probably everyone thought he and his crew were trash, but even with half his crew cutting out early and taking their shares, he, Bash, and Clinton did all right for themselves, thanks to Bash's instincts for the market and care with investments.

Bash was also the one who'd dug every bullet out of his body when the poachers had gotten to him. He hadn't said a word, just reached Harrison first, settled him back, and went to work with this look on his face like he would be good-goddamned if he was going to lose his alpha that day. That was the night Bash had called him his best friend and went to battle with three members of the crew whose animals were scrambling to take Harrison out for alpha when he was too weak to do it himself. He was here because of Bash, but that bear didn't like mush and compliments. The best gift Harrison could give him for his loyalty was permission to claim a mate and bring her into the park. Bash wanted nothing more, and now, Harrison felt that yearning, too.

Audrey had changed everything.

Yesterday had been one of the best days of his life. He'd become hopeful. His burden had been lightened when he'd laid some of it on her shoulders, and she was a strong woman. She had carried that load with grace and had given him the same advice Creed and Tagan, alpha of the Ashe Crew, had been trying to tell him for months. But it all had made more sense when she'd said it.

He'd found his queen, and that thought scared the shit out of him and excited him at the same time.

Go after the life you want.

Harrison killed the chainsaw and clipped out, "Bash! Clinton! Let's call it a day."

"Yeah, boss," Bash said, like he did every time a shift ended.

Wordlessly, Clinton turned his chainsaw off then pulled his earmuffs off his head and settled them around his neck.

"Six hundred forty-three," Bash reported in, wiping the sweat of his brow on his arm as he caught up to Harrison. "Pathetic. Damon won't be happy. We're holding up the Ashe Crew's next jobsite. At this rate"—he swung his gaze down the mountain and tallied in his head—"they'll be sittin' around for a week before we have this place cleared for them."

Harrison made a ticking sound. He hated letting the dragon down. Hated. It. Damon had done so much for the inhabitants of his mountains, and he deserved the best from every crew. The Boarlanders weren't pulling their weight. "We'll have Kirk and Mason with us tomorrow, and we'll work until sundown. We'll catch back up as best we can, but for now, I have to be there when the new crew members move in, and I need to talk to you and Clinton."

"Crew meeting?" Bash asked, his jet-black eyebrows jacking up.

Harrison ducked his chin once and switched his chainsaw to his other hand as he climbed over the freshly cut trees on the steep hillside toward his truck.

"Crew meeting!" Bash called to Clinton, who was falling behind.

"Yeah, I heard," he muttered.

Clinton was going to lose his crap today, but this had been coming for a long time.

Harrison lowered his tailgate and set his chainsaw in its case while Clinton and Bash did the same with theirs. He peeled off his sweat-soaked white T-shirt and tossed it in the back before he pulled a clean one out of a duffle bag he kept stocked. Clinton didn't bother with a clean shirt, as though he expected an uncontrolled Change, which was exactly why Harrison nixed Bash calling shotgun. He made Clinton sit up front instead. If he was going to Change, Harrison had big plans to boot his ass out of his truck, and quick.

"This is about Audrey," Clinton said in a subdued tone as Harrison jammed the key in the ignition.

"It's about a lot of things. Mostly, we need to talk about what we're doing and where we're going."

"Why? We're fine the way we are."

"Are we?" Bash asked in a dark tone from the back seat. "I'm not. I know for certain Harrison's not happy. He lost his whole damned crew, Clinton."

"Are you happy?" Harrison asked. "Answer me honestly, because I can't imagine anyone with as big a chip on their shoulder as you is really finding joy in their life."

"No," Clinton murmured, "I'm not happy."

"It's been hard, and for a long time. Can we all agree on that?" Harrison asked.

"Yes," Clinton and Bash answered.

"I'm lifting the ban on women in the trailer park."

"Harrison—" Clinton interrupted.

"No, you'll listen. Your time for talking and sabotaging is through. I'd made that rule a long time ago because some of my bears weren't ready to treat a woman with respect, and I didn't want to put some frail human woman at risk in my park. My crew needed time to mature. It was never a permanent rule, Clinton, and I was ready to lift it right as you came to me, begging to be a Boarlander. Because you were so opposed to women in our park, I held off on lifting the ban. Was I right to do it? Hell, I don't know. Maybe if I'd done this sooner, I could've kept some of my boys. Or maybe not. I can't change what's been done, but I can do my best to guide what we have left to a better future. I want us happy."

"But women in this park won't make me happy," Clinton said, staring out the window.

"Why? Just tell me the reason why so I can understand why you've pushed everyone so hard."

"Because I'm cursed, Harrison. You think I'm doing this to hurt us? Because I hate women?" Clinton looked sick and shook his head. "I drag hell with me wherever I go. I don't want any more women hurt because of me."

Well, that was the realest answer he'd ever heard from Clinton.

"You ain't cursed, and we ain't destined to

be miserable the rest of our lives, Clinton. I'm lifting the ban—"

"You're making a mistake."

"It's my mistake to make!" Harrison yelled. "I let you run this crew too long, and you know what happens when a low-ranking bear runs things? The whole damned hierarchy breaks down. I put up with too much. I did it because I saw what Creed was doing with his troubled bears, and I thought you would come around if I was a good enough alpha, but you never did. You got worse. I've called Audrey, and she'll be waiting at the park—"

"Dammit, Harrison—"

"I'm not done," he barked, turning onto a sharp switchback. From here, he could see the park in the valley below. "Ladies are now allowed in the park, and Bash, I'm gonna need you to order some supplies."

"For what, boss?"

"We're fixing up the place because we let our home go, boys. That place is a crap-hole. I'm embarrassed to bring Mason and Kirk and Audrey there. Our crew is going through an overhaul, and part of that is improving our territory so that it's safe and inviting for mates, and someday, God-willing, cubs. I mean, for fuck's sake, the Grayland Mobile

Park looks pristine. And they're *Gray Backs*. I want that for us. I want a fire pit, a gathering place, a grilling area, a work-out space, a damned swing-set in the back, all of it."

"I want a door," Bash said helpfully.

"Yeah, I don't really know why you haven't put a new one on. It's been two weeks since you kicked it down."

"Because Clinton," Bash muttered.

"Okay, also, you two need to settle the issue of who is my Second. We need a pecking order, and it needs to stick."

Clinton had gone quiet, arms crossed tightly over his chest like he was shutting down. "I have nowhere else to go."

"Then don't go anywhere. I don't want to lose you, Clinton."

"This is because of Audrey. She's making you shake up a system that doesn't need to change."

"Look, Audrey is mine."

"After a few days," Clinton scoffed.

"And how fast did it take for you to know with your mates, Clinton? Huh? How long until you bonded?"

Clinton jerked a furious gaze to Harrison, then back out the window.

"I called your alpha from a few crews ago.

Can't you see it's not fair that you got to try to build a family, but Bash and I never get that chance?"

When Clinton huffed a furious breath, the air stank of fur, but he needed to hear this. Needed to accept what was happening.

"How long?" Harrison demanded.

Clinton swallowed audibly. "It was instant."

Harrison's stomach clenched at the pain that had tainted Clinton's voice.

"Holy shit," Bash whispered.

"Audrey is my mate. I didn't expect it, wasn't looking for one, but my bear chose her, and I'm going to work hard to get her to choose me back. She will be a part of this if she wants to be. She makes me happy, and it's been a long damned time. I deserve for things to go better, and I'm going to work my ass off for life to be better for the both of you. You're all the crew I've got. From here on, I promise, I'm going to do my best to dig us out of this hole."

"I'm in," Bash said, gripping Harrison's shoulder from behind.

"Clinton?" Harrison asked.

But Clinton only sighed the saddest sound and stared out the window at the passing evergreens. As they pulled into the back entrance of Boarland Mobile Park, Clinton said, "You're a good alpha, Harrison."

But Harrison hadn't missed it. That wasn't really a declaration of fealty.

Clinton had given a compliment for the first time since Harrison had met him, but it sounded an awful lot like a goodbye.

NINE

On Harrison's porch stairs, Audrey drew her knees up closer to her chest so she could rest the paperwork onto her legs to read it. Today was a tank top and cutoff jean shorts kind of day, so she smiled at the memory of being offered a job at Moosey's Bait and Barbecue. She hadn't exactly been dressed for an interview. Moosey's was nestled in the mountains, located about half an hour before Boarland Mobile Park. Since she was getting here way early and on an empty stomach, she'd stopped in and bought a brisket sandwich.

The joint had been busy, but the owner, Joey Dorsey, had sat down at her table and asked if she had any experience with the service industry. They'd talked for a while, and then he'd brought her an application and told her he was looking for a new full-time server.

The only problem was her confusion on where she fit in this place. Her hotel was down in Saratoga, and she wasn't about to beg a trailer here. Not with Clinton so volatile.

Last night, after Aviana and Beaston had said she would hurt Clinton, she'd gotten a sick feeling deep in her gut as Harrison had driven her back to the hotel. Clinton and Bash had been silent in the backseat of the truck, but the alpha had talked on happily and held her hand.

She would hurt him if she left here and went back to Buffalo Gap, but she was beginning to think she would hurt him worse if she stayed. Audrey didn't want to be the last fissure that shattered the frail foundation of the Boarlanders.

The throaty rumble of a car sounded from far off, and her pulse quickened with the thought of seeing Harrison again. Today had felt like the longest day of her life. From the second she'd gotten a call from him earlier, she'd been so ready to feel his arms around her so he could banish all her melancholy thoughts about leaving.

She wouldn't tell him about the job offer at Moosey's. They weren't ready for her to put down roots like that yet, so she jogged over to her Jeep and shoved the application in the glovebox.

The vehicle wasn't Harrison's, though. Instead, a classic, forest green Mustang with black racing stripes roared under the Missionary Impossible sign.

She hooked her hand on her hip and waved to the smiling familiar face behind the wheel. Kirk pulled to a stop, his brakes not even letting off a squeak. This was a shifter who took good care of his old muscle car. The dark-eyed man with the longer hair rolled down the window and rested his arm on the ledge. Yanking his sunglasses off, he looked her up and down. "I know you. I saw you at the bar the other night."

"I'm Audrey," she introduced herself, offering her hand for a shake.

She liked that he didn't give her a limp handshake like some men did.

"Kirk, honorary Boarlander." He released his firm grip on her palm, then ducked his gaze under his lowered sun visor and whistled at the dilapidated park.

"It could use some work," she said, scrunching up her nose. "Harrison and the boys aren't off their shift yet, but I can help you move your stuff if you want."

Kirk sniffed the air. "Are you a shifter?"

With a cheeky grin, she said, "Maybe."

"Hmm. And you swear you aren't just being polite? You don't mind moving me in?"

"Nah, it'll give me something to do while I wait."

"Sa-weet." Kirk pulled up a piece of scribbled paper and scanned it quick. "I'm in trailer six."

Squinting, Audrey pointed at the first trailer on the left, directly across the gravel road from Harrison's. The number six had disappeared off the siding near the broken porch light, but the chipped paint still showed the discolored outline of the number. "There she be. At least you have a door."

"Well, that is a bright side, I guess," Kirk said with a good-natured chuckle.

She liked him already. At least he wasn't pitching a tantrum at moving into an ancient singlewide with weed landscaping.

He took a wide birth and backed onto the cracked concrete pad in front of trailer six. He hadn't brought much, just enough boxes to fill his back seat and trunk, so she stacked two of them in her arms and followed him up the sagging porch stairs and through the waterlogged front door. The inside, like Harrison's, surprised her. It was clean and fixed up. Even the floors felt sturdy where she'd expected them to be rotted straight through. Also like Harrison's trailer, there was a kitchen on the left, a bedroom beyond that, and a large living room that took up the space on the right side.

"It's better than I expected," Kirk murmured. "Set the boxes down over there, if you don't mind," he directed her, twitching his chin to a two-seater couch. "I'll unpack them later."

By the time Kirk's belongings were unloaded into the living room, the sound of Harrison's truck echoed through the valley, and something much bigger, too. An eighteen wheeler, perhaps.

Harrison pulled his giant pickup in front of his trailer and locked eyes immediately with her. He'd looked troubled, almost pained the instant before, but as she jogged down Kirk's stairs, his lips curved into a stunning smile.

She ran to him and caught him just as he got out. He hugged her tight and lifted her feet off the ground, then angled his head and kissed her like he hadn't seen her in a week instead of just a day. *Just a day.* That term didn't mean the same as it did a week ago, when each day looked just like the next, and just like the one before.

If she left him, it would hurt deeply.

"I missed you," she admitted in an emotional whisper.

He drew back and cupped her face, his brows lowering, worry pooling in his eyes. "What's wrong?"

Her voice would tremble, so she shook her head and kissed him again. The noise from the eighteen-wheeler was deafening now against her oversensitive ears, so she covered them with her palms as Harrison shook Kirk's hand and pulled him in for a mannish hug and resounding back clap. She was glad he was much gentler with her.

The big rig came into view as Bash and Clinton filed out of Harrison's Chevy, and together, they stared in confusion as a truck pulling an old singlewide trailer behind it rumbled slowly through the park. With the hiss of brakes, the massive semi came to a stop in front of them, and Beaston rolled down the window. "I come bearing gifts."

A dark-headed man leaned over and gave a two fingered wave.

"Hey, Mason," Harrison said. He eyed the

mobile home Beaston was dragging. "You know we have a trailer for you here, right?"

"Oh, this isn't for Mason," Beaston said. "My alpha and the alpha of the Ashe Crew are giving this to you."

"To me?" Harrison asked.

"No." Beaston jammed a finger at Audrey. "It's a gift for her."

Mason hopped out of the passenger's side of the truck, and Beaston pulled on through.

Stunned, Audrey looked at the old cream-colored mobile home with its dark shutters and painted red door. It looked like a squirrel had tried to chew a hole through it to get in. But when she saw the crooked numbers by the doorframe, *1010*, chills blasted across her arms. She rubbed her hands over her forearms to warm herself up, and beside her, the tall, dark-eyed boar shifter gave her an odd, knowing smile.

"That old trailer is magic. Take good care of her, and she'll take good care of you."

"Oh, but I don't live here."

"Uh, I actually wanted to talk to you about that," Harrison said, his frown still following the progress of the trailer to the end of the road.

"Do you want to be a Boarlander?" Bash

asked excitedly and way too loud.

"Bash!" Harrison reprimanded.

"Sorry."

Audrey giggled and pressed her cool palms against her cheeks.

Rolling his eyes heavenward, Harrison muttered, "Excuse us for a minute." He gripped her elbow, then led her closer to his trailer and away from the others.

"Look, I asked you to come by for a reason. That hotel you're staying in is thirty-five bucks a night. That's over a thousand dollars a month, and I know you can't stick around and keep paying that." Harrison stepped closer and pulled her hands away from her face. He gripped her fingers as he smiled and lowered his voice. "And every time I think about you leaving, I get this panicky feeling, like I'd be losing a piece of me that I only just found, you know? I'm not asking you to move in with me or to pledge under me. I know it's too early for that, but I want you here. For a day or for a week. I'll take whatever time you're willing to give me."

"But I don't know if I belong here. I'm different than you and the others, Harrison. I'm a tiger, not a lumberjack werebear."

"And he's a gorilla," Harrison said, pointing

to Kirk, "and he's a boar." He pointed to Mason. "And I'm yours. I'm asking you to stay, Audrey. Here. With me. You don't have to pledge to my crew. Just…stay."

"In ten-ten," she said on a breath as she looked at where Beaston was settling it at the end of the road. It did look inviting with the pink sunset and piney mountains behind it.

Harrison cupped her cheek and kissed her, then eased back by inches. "I wish I could give you more, but this is all I have—a shitty old trailer park, a half-crazed crew of idiots, and this." He pressed her palm against his chest, right over his drumming heartbeat.

"But what about Clinton?"

"I already talked to him about the changes that will be happening. About you." Sadness washed through his eyes. "Clinton will have to be fine with it."

But when Audrey looked for Clinton, he wasn't anywhere to be seen.

Harrison sighed. "He'll get used to this. Just like you, Kirk, and Mason will have to adjust to life here. Clinton doesn't like change, but I have to fix things, and it won't happen without a complete shake-up. You're part of that. Not the hard part. The good part." Harrison grinned and dropped down to one knee.

"What are you doing, ridiculous man. Get up."

"I'm on my knees, begging you, kitty. Pick this place. Pick me."

Her eyes prickled with tears as she looked around Harrison's dilapidated trailer park.

This could be her home. This could be where she grew her roots deep and strong.

She could be happy here.

Dashing her knuckles under her eye to catch a tear, she nodded. "Okay."

Harrison stood in a blur and cupped her neck, pressed his lips against hers. She'd thought because of the growl in his throat he would be rough, but his mouth moved surprisingly gently over hers. As he eased away and rested his forehead on hers, he whispered, "I'll make you happy here, Audrey. I'll give you a good crew, I promise."

And she heard it. That strong, steady tone that he'd told her to listen for.

Down to her marrow, she knew that Harrison—*her Harrison*—was telling the truth.

TEN

Audrey ducked out of the way as Mason hustled out of 1010 with an armload of lumber. Beaston had settled the old trailer on a concrete pad at the end of the road, facing the entrance, and overlooking the rest of the park.

"Oh, sorry," she murmured, dodging Bash as he filed out of 1010 balancing an impressive stack of what looked and smelled like fresh cut two-by-sixes.

Bash adjusted the stack and ruffled her hair as he walked by, his grin catching. At least one of the Boarlanders was happy she was here. Clinton was still nowhere to be seen.

"Ten-ten looks best with a deck," Beaston said from right behind her.

Audrey jumped and clutched her chest. Thanks to her animal, she wasn't often snuck up on, but Beaston was scary quiet.

He stood right behind her with his arms clasped behind his back. "I want to help build it for you, but I have to get back to Ana. She's pregnant." Pride tinged the last part.

"I know. I felt the baby move last night, remember?"

"Yeah, I just like saying it. She's having my raven boy. I don't like to be away from her."

She ducked her smile. Beaston always sounded snarly unless he was talking about his Ana. Then his voice went all soft.

"We'll build the deck," she said. "You go on back to your mate and tell her 'hi' from me."

Beaston jerked his head in a nod and turned for the now empty big rig, waiting in the middle of the gravel road.

"Beaston?" she asked.

He turned with a frown on his face. "What?"

With a sigh, she approached and put her arms around his shoulders carefully. "Thank you."

Beaston froze under her hug. "For what?"

"For helping me get to Harrison at Sammy's bar last week. For bringing ten-ten." She squeezed harder. "For seeing more than other people do."

Beaston softened and lifted his hands to her back, then pulled her close for a moment. Head cocked and green eyes blazing, he gave her a half smile and walked away. Over his shoulder, he asked, "Do you like knives?"

"Uuuh," she stumbled. "I used to carry a pocket knife."

He climbed up the eighteen-wheeler and hung from the door. "Good," he murmured just before he climbed in behind the wheel. He stuck his head out the window. "I almost forgot. Nards lives in ten-ten. Don't hurt him." Engine roaring, the truck drove slowly away and back under the park sign. Beaston was a bit of a wild bear, and an odd one, too, but she liked him.

Harrison wrapped his arms around her from behind and rested his chin on top of her head as they watched the truck disappear through the trees. "You ready to see your trailer?"

The boys were going in and out like a line of worker ants, but she and Harrison ducked inside between them. Kirk grinned as he scooped the last bunch of wood. "There she is. Queen of the trailer park, queen of our hearts."

Audrey snorted and crouched down when Kirk swung the wood wide to angle it toward the door. When he left, only she and Harrison remained. He shut the door gently and watched her face with an expression that said it mattered what she thought of this place.

The walls were painted white, and the dark laminate wood floors under her feet felt a little squishy. The couch, kitchen table, and chairs were all bound together for the journey in the middle of the living room, and to the left, a white-washed country kitchen with faux wood countertops bisected the living space and a bedroom. She giggled at a miniature refrigerator that took up roughly a third of the space for a full-sized one.

"We'll get you a big one," Harrison promised.

"This one is fine for now. It's just me in here. This place is a lot bigger than I thought."

"Yeah, you'll have the biggest trailer in the park."

"My castle," she murmured, glowing from the inside out with pleasure.

The kitchen was full of boxes, all bound together, and when she opened one, there were dishes packed neatly. When she meandered through the kitchen, touching the smooth countertop as she went, and made her way into the bedroom, she was shocked into stillness, right there in the doorway. The bedroom was huge. It had a built-in dresser and a queen-size bed. The mattress was bare, but a stack of sheets and a thick cream and blue floral comforter was folded neatly in the middle and bound with thick twine. The linens smelled good, like fresh breeze laundry detergent, and as she made her way to the bathroom on the other side, she couldn't contain her grin. There was a washer and a dryer inside, right across from the sink.

"You like it?" Harrison asked.

"This is going to sound silly, but I haven't had my own washer and dryer before. When I moved out of my dad's trailer, I was living in this tiny apartment that didn't have hookups, so I've used a Laundromat for years." With a happy sigh, she turned and leaned on the door frame. "I love it." She looked up at the slightly sagging ceiling and shrugged. "I can't explain it, but this place feels homey to me."

"You're an amazing woman, Audrey," Harrison said from where he rested his hip against the built-in dresser. "I never imagined a lady would be okay living out here in my park. Not the way it is."

Audrey made her way to the bed and untied the linens. "Yeah, well, I can see the potential. I feel like I'm coming in right on the cusp of huge changes. It's exciting that I'll be here to see what you do with this park. With your people."

"You feel like my people, too," Harrison said low, eyes on the sheets as he helped her to cover the mattress.

Dragons flapped around in her belly at his admission, and she had to bite back her grin because he looked so serious and lost in thought right now. She snuck glances at him as they made the bed. His powerful arms flexed against his thin white T-shirt, and she could make out the definition of his muscular chest. His thick neck led up to a two-day sexy scruff on his jaw, and his eyes were that dark evening blue that she'd fallen in love with. There was a cut on his forearm, but it was already healed and the thin line of blood dried, and his hair was all mussed, likely from the hardhat he wore on his shift. Bed made, she jumped up and landed starfish-style on the plush mattress. For an old trailer, the Ashe Crew and Gray Backs hadn't skimped on furnishings. This bed would be like sleeping on a cloud.

"I make a nest every night," she admitted.

"Like a bird?" Harrison asked, amusement

in his tone as he lay down beside her.

"No, like a badass tiger. I pile pillows all around me. That's what makes me feel safe enough to sleep. I'm a light sleeper because I hear everything. Did you know my hearing is even better than yours? I researched it."

Harrison chuckled and pulled her in close. "That sucks."

"What I'm saying is, maybe you don't have to bear all the burden of making sure this place is safe at night."

Harrison frowned at her and plucked absently at a wayward strand of hair that had fallen against her cheek. "What do you mean?"

Audrey rested her chin against his chest so she could see his face better. "I mean, I can help you patrol the territory if you want. Then you can sleep more."

He smiled sadly down at her, stroking her hair. "I don't think it works like that."

"Harrison, I won't let anyone hurt you," she whispered. "You're mine to protect, too."

His heart thumped faster against her chin as he searched her eyes. Then slowly, he pulled her hand under the hem of his T-shirt and up, up until her fingertips brushed four raised claw-mark scars. "I was ten when I got this."

"Oh, Harrison," she murmured, heart aching. "Why did he do it?"

"Because he drank, and booze made him angry and bitter. It made him blame his problems on anything but himself, and I was an easy mark. I was asleep...fuck." Harrison jerked his gaze to the window and shook his head over and over again. "I've never talked about this stuff."

She would *not* cry. She wouldn't. He was being strong, and so would she. Audrey pushed his shirt up and over his head, then kissed the long scars one by one.

Harrison swallowed hard and murmured, "I was asleep, and I woke up with my dad's raging grizzly over me. I couldn't Change fast enough, and even when I did, I was half his size. I fought, but I was hurt and scared, trying to just get out of the house. I wanted to get out into the woods where I had a chance at getting away."

"And did you?"

"Yeah, but I was injured, and it was winter. I was so cold. I spent the night out there thinking I wouldn't heal fast enough. That I was going to bleed out alone, and I remember staring at the sky and cursing my mom for leaving. For dying. I was so angry at everything. I made a rule that night to protect myself. If I lived, I would never let my dad in again. I would tolerate him, but harden myself until I was old enough to leave and find a crew. I would fight back. That night was the first time I'd ever defended myself, and in order to save my bear from being broken, I had to let him fight instead of just lying there, waiting for my dad to get tired of hurting me. And I did. Those were the last permanent scars he ever left on me."

But Harrison was wrong. His dad had done something worse than scar his skin. He'd scarred his insides so that Harrison couldn't sleep like he should. So that Harrison couldn't feel safe. He'd battered his naturally protective instincts until they were barely manageable. His dad had made it to where even after all these years, he was still a hindrance in Harrison's ability to function normally.

A low growl reverberated through her as she rested her cheek against the claw mark. She hated his father for what he'd done. She ran the flat of her tongue down the length of the mark, then froze as her gaze locked onto his. "I'm sorry," she rushed out, lurching away from him. "I don't know why I did that."

His face cracked into a slow grin. "You

smell like fur."

Mortified, she sat up and clamped her arms around her stomach. "My animal thinks if she licks stuff, it fixes the problem, but my human side knows that's stupid because your scar is already healed," she rambled. "You taste good. I'm sorry for doing that. I should go."

"Stop, stop, stop," he murmured, his eyes glinting with a sexy wickedness. He pulled her head gently toward his chest. "Do it again. I like feeling your tongue on me."

She hesitated an instant, then stuck out the tip of her tongue and licked his scar again.

"Like you mean it, kitty."

Ooooh, he was sexy, demanding in his deep voice that she expose her animal instincts like this.

She slid her hand between his legs just to feel him, and sure enough, his erection was already hard as a rock and ready. Feeling much braver, she licked his scar again, then kissed down his ribcage. At his hipbone, she bit him hard enough that he jerked his pelvis and rolled his eyes closed.

Harrison was so reactive, her confidence grew, and now she had that same numb, happy feeling she'd gotten the first time they were intimate. She didn't stifle the purr in her throat as she kissed his tense abs and pulled his jeans down his hips, unsheathing him completely.

God, he was stunning. His long dick throbbed once between his powerful legs, and now his fingers were in her hair, pushing her farther down until her lips brushed the swollen head of his cock. His muscles tensed as she licked the salty drop of moisture at the tip. So good. She loved this, loved how pliable he became with every touch of her lips, loved the taste of him, loved that he was barely in control. *Mine, mine, mine.*

Audrey rolled her hips against his leg as she slid her mouth over his cock. More. She needed so much more. Releasing him, she shimmied out of her cut-off shorts and pulled her tank top over her head.

Harrison's eyes were bright now, like fresh snow. "Come here," he rumbled.

She crawled over him and straddled his hips, then kissed him. How insane that a big, dominant alpha grizzly shifter would allow her to be on top, controlling their pace. The purr in her throat grew louder, then softer, then louder again.

With a devilish grin, Harrison gripped her

hips and slid down the bed under her until his face was between her straddled legs.

"What are you—oooh," she groaned as he lifted up and sucked gently on her clit.

When Harrison slipped his tongue up her wet slit, her hips jerked. He licked her again, and she swayed forward and closed her eyes. He teased her again and again, tongue hesitating at her entrance before he sucked her clit.

"Harrison, please," she begged, voice growly and unrecognizable. Maybe she would be embarrassed by her animal side later when Harrison's clever mouth wasn't on her.

Sliding her legs farther apart, she lowered down for him and rocked her hips with the pace he set. So much pressure growing with every lick. When Harrison's tongue dipped shallowly into her, she gasped his name.

His hand brushed down her back as she arched for him, and now his needy growl was rattling against her sex. His tongue slid deep inside her, and she groaned, tossing her head back at how good he felt right there. She was going to come soon, but she didn't want to finish like this.

"I want you inside of me," she whispered. The tingling sensation was growing so intensely now. So close.

Harrison sat up on the edge of the bed, taking her with him. His teeth were on her neck as she settled over his thick shaft, sliding over him slowly. Her chest heaved as she bowed against him and offered him better access to her neck. Harrison moved within her, powerful body flexing with every graceful stroke. His arms were strong around her back, dragging her closer every time their hips met.

"Audrey," he rasped out through gritted teeth.

Harrison froze and warmth pulsed into her the second the first throbbing sensation of her climax burst through her. Harrison pulled her down hard over him, again and again as her orgasm became more intense, more consuming. His dick thumped against her insides as he emptied himself.

His muscles relaxed as her body pulsed on with faint, delicious aftershocks. Harrison massaged the back of her neck as she moved languidly against him, and when she finally stilled, he angled his face and kissed her.

She thought he would lay them back, but he seemed content to just hold her like this. And as his kiss gentled, he hugged her tighter against his chest. Burying his face against her neck, he murmured, "What are you doing to me, woman?"

Audrey ran gentle nails up and down his back as he rocked her gently. This wasn't a quick bang followed by a rush to leave. Harrison was coveting her body and making sure she knew she was cared for after the intimacy they'd just shared. His lips were soft against her neck as he told her without words how much he adored her.

He was so warm, so strong against her. What was she doing to him? "I'm loving you."

Harrison paused and eased back, searched her eyes as he cupped her cheek. His gaze ducked to her lips, and he sighed. "Soon, I want you to come with me when I walk the property line, but I can feel you holding back. I can still see shame in the color of your cheeks when your animal exerts herself. Give me your animal side, and I'll show you my woods."

"If I show you my secret self, you'll let me in?" she whispered.

The corner of his lips lifted in a faint smile. "Accept your tiger, and you can have anything you want."

ELEVEN

"You sound happy, baby," Dad said over the cell phone.

Audrey smiled down at the Boarland Mobile Park, newly lit with strands of outdoor lights. She'd climbed up the hill behind 1010 to get some privacy to call her dad, and below, she could see Harrison's little kingdom. Her kingdom now, too. Harrison and Kirk were playing a game of horseshoes, and the echo of their trash talk traveled up to her.

Three days living here, and her old life felt so far away. "I really am happy, Dad. I just wanted to thank you for being so amazing to me when I was growing up." Harrison's inner scars from his abusive father ran deep, and she'd been thinking about how lucky she was to be born to a good man. "You are a really good dad. I don't think anyone else would've encouraged me to move out of state and find a crew like this. And you did it without a single thought for yourself."

"Well, honey, that's what daddies do. It broke my heart to see you go. Part of me hoped you would turn right back around and come home to me. But a bigger part of me wanted you to find a place where you fit. As much as I wanted it to be true, you didn't fit in Buffalo Gap. Swear to come visit me, though."

Audrey laughed thickly and drew a circle in the dirt between her legs with a crooked stick. "I swear. And as soon as you can, I want you to come up here and see me and these crazy boys I'm living around. They're wild, but good people. I think you'll like them." She frowned at Clinton's trailer where he sat by himself drinking a beer. Well, most of them.

Another wave of pain seized her muscles, and she doubled over and grunted.

"Audrey? Are you okay?"

"Yeah, it's just the animal," she gritted out.

Sympathetically, he asked, "She's close?"

"Yeah. It's been a while."

"Do the other shifters hurt like you?"

"I don't know. We don't talk about that stuff."

"Well, you're there with people just like

you. Maybe you should."

Audrey forced her stiffened muscles to relax as best she could and shifted her attention to Harrison. Maybe he felt her watching from the night shadows of the trees because he lifted his face and locked his gaze right where she was sitting.

"Maybe I will. I love you, dad."

"I love you, too, honey. You call me again soon."

"I will. Goodnight."

"'Night."

She ended the call and stared at the glowing cell phone screen until it went dark.

Tomorrow was a big day. It was the first day of her new job at Moosey's, and she didn't want an uncontrolled Change with all the stress. No way in hell did she want a repeat of her eighth birthday party. But Harrison had a lot on his plate right now with bringing a new crew in line, hitting lumber numbers, and fixing up the park.

She felt bad asking about things she should already know, and Harrison was already being drained from all sides. She didn't want to be part of the problem.

But...

If she didn't ask, she would never

understand her animal.

A long, low snarl rattled her throat as she doubled over again. This was her least favorite part of being a shifter. This right here was why it had been so easy to hate her mom. It wasn't the leaving that had destroyed any loyalty Audrey had for her. It was the fact she put an uncontrollable beast inside of her, and then left the animal to eat her up.

The pain became blinding, and Audrey lurched forward to retch. She was scared. That was a part of sharing her body with a monster. Fear. She was scared of the animal, scared of the pain of the Change. Hers wasn't fast like Harrison and Clinton's had been. It wasn't explosive or instant. It was slow and drawn out, and sometimes it stalled, and she just lay there, dying, caught between one form and the other, broken and wishing she could cry out in agony.

Sharing this part of herself would hurt the incredible relationship she was building with a man she was falling deeply in love with. She imagined him looking down at her hideous transformation with disgust crooking his lips, like all those crowds that had gathered around her limp body on the pavement. A flash of police sirens and the sting of the tranquilizer dart flashed across her mind. She'd been able to see everything from the burning pavement where she'd fallen. Every face in the crowd, every flash of every camera. She hadn't been able to move a muscle, but she'd heard the horror and revulsion in everyone's tone as they'd looked at her shifted body.

Now she was terrified to let anyone else see her.

"You're fighting her," Harrison said from behind her.

With a gasp, Audrey twisted around. "Don't look at me," she rasped.

Hurt flashed across Harrison's face as he took a step back. He smelled like fur, and his eyes reflected like an animal's in the glow of the trailer park below them.

"I'm sorry. I'm sorry," she panted, gripping clumps of grass in her fists. She was on her hands and knees, buckling under the pain. "I don't know how to do this. Everything hurts." The last syllable turned into a feral sounding growl. "I'm scared." Tears streamed down her face, and she wished she was stronger. Braver. Better. Harrison deserved that.

"Listen to me, Audrey. Fighting her will make it so much worse. You've been waiting too long, making her force her way out of you.

Give in." He was so close now, not touching her, but she could feel his warmth. He was kneeling in front of her. Dangerous.

"I don't want to hurt you."

"You won't. Look at me." Harrison leveled her with a bright-eyed look. "We'll do this together. I'll Change with you. I'll show you my territory. Just give her your body."

"I don't know hooooooow," she cried as her arm snapped.

"Fuck, Audrey! You'll drag it out. Just close your eyes and give in!"

A smattering of sickening pops sounded, and two massive bear paws landed on either side of her, so hard the earth shook beneath her. He bellowed a deafening sound right above her, and the monster in her middle responded with a long, echoing roar that shook the air like thunder.

Squeezing her eyes closed against the fire lapping at every cell in her body, Audrey relaxed her muscles and reached for the tiger. Thirty counted seconds of agony later, she lay panting and limp. Harrison's massive, chestnut grizzly paced frantically in front of her, as if he'd endured the agony of her Change right along with her.

Thirty seconds. Sure, it was no explosive

Change like Harrison had accomplished, but it was a record for her.

She was scared to get up, scared she would lose her mind and attack the bear she loved, but as the seconds ticked by, all she felt was adoration for him. He looked so worried, her Harrison.

He paced closer and buried his nose against the scruff of her neck. Warmth spread through her from where he touched her fur. Struggling upward, she held her head up and twitched her tail as Harrison curled around her protectively. With a hard blink, she looked down at her lithe body. Usually, she hated herself most in this form, but tonight was different. Perhaps it was because this past week the Boarlanders and Gray Backs had seemed so excited that she was a tiger. Or maybe it was Harrison, who seemed completely enamored with her any time she let a purr slip. But if felt like more. Like maybe the change was because she saw herself differently now. She wasn't a freak. She just wasn't human. It didn't make her an abomination. It just made her different, and maybe different was okay. It made her fit in just fine with these people, who she was growing to adore.

Something large moved in the woods below them, and a quick drumming from above startled her into a crouched position. She hissed out a warming, placing herself in front of Harrison. But when she looked up into the branches to see what had made that terrifying noise, a huge silverback gorilla sat propped on a thick branch, hand clutched onto the trunk of the tree. Kirk. He climbed down gracefully and circled her. When he reached out and brushed her fur with one curled, dark finger, she tensed, but allowed it.

A low rumble rattled Harrison's chest behind her, and Kirk backed away. He stood frozen, propped up on his powerful arms, and behind him, a shockingly massive ink-black boar with long white tusks trotted forward. Farther back, another titan grizzly with fur the color of pitch ambled through the trees. They were all watching her with wary eyes. Wary, not disgusted.

She pushed herself up, ears back, tail low, because she was the smallest animal here, but at her movement, the others backed away a few paces. All but Harrison. She bared her teeth and let off a roar, then let it taper to a long growl just to test her voice.

Harrison nuzzled his face down her

ribcage, and Kirk beat his chest again. Mason kicked up dirt under his front hoof, and Bash's bear stood on his hind legs like he wanted to see her better. It was Harrison who moved off first, pausing every few steps to look back at her.

Right. She should follow.

Bash settled in behind her, but Kirk and Mason made their way side by side through the woods near them. The earth was warm and moist against the thick pads of her paws, and captured by a moment of excitement, she took off running, using her tail for balance. Crouching down in front of Harrison, she leapt at him and wrapped her claws around his neck, then gave him a gentle play bite. He didn't flinch away or act like her claws hurt. Instead, he grunted and kept walking, dragging her along with him.

She released him and ran her tongue along the side of his face, then stopped and cleaned a sticker burr from her own paw. Bash pushed his nose against her back, then meandered around her with powerful strides.

She'd shifted…with other shifters! This was awesome!

Audrey took off again, this time toward Kirk, but he was having none of her shenanigans, and he scrambled up a tree and out of her way. Leaping through the air, she caught the trunk and held on, a few feet above the ground, and all of her claws dug deep into the bark. She could chase Kirk, but Harrison let off a short roar, demanding her attention, like when his bear had called her tiger out of her. Magic mate.

Audrey followed, but not before she raked her claws down the trunk. *My tree.*

She ran to catch up. Behind her, Kirk's massive body hit the ground and began to follow them again. Bash's giant ass was a fantastic target for biting, so she bunched her muscles, then pounced and gnawed on his stump tail, her claws in his thick hide. Bash grunted and turned and swatted her off. Didn't hurt. Her giant paws sank in a mud skid as she trotted beside him. She hated when her fur got dirty. She should clean it. No, Harrison was too far ahead, and she wanted to snuggle. Ignoring the instinct to stop and run her tongue over her paws, she bolted and caught up with her mate. *Mine.* With a deep, rumbling purr, she rubbed herself up the side of his body, the wrong way up his fur. That would've driven her nuts, but Harrison only gave her an affectionate look over his muscular shoulder.

I love him. I love everyone. Had she ever been this happy? *Nope. Hi, Mason!* She took off toward the giant boar, but he skittered out of her way, then spun and aggressively lowered his tusks at her. *Eee.* She pulled off her hunt to save her hide and bolted for Harrison again.

Sky, stars, trees, dirt. She loved this place. This was paradise. Below was ten-ten. *Ten-ten, my den.* She sneezed a tiger laugh. *Witty kitty. Pretty kitty.* Audrey arched her back and stretched her paws in front of her so she could admire her stripes. She'd hated them before—but how ridiculous. At least she wasn't a werebeaver. When she straightened up, she roared happily from the diaphragm, and Harrison answered, then Bash.

Below, Clinton yelled, "Shut up! I'm tryin' to sleep!"

Grumpy bear. She should play-bite him. But when she trotted down toward the park, Harrison cut her off and twitched his head toward the east. Fine. Later. Later she would play-bite Clinton and make him like her.

For now, she was content to follow Harrison and see where he always disappeared to at night before he went to sleep. This was his gift to her for being a good little shifter.

He was sharing his ritual. Sharing his compulsion.

She would follow this trail later with her camera and take pictures for her scrapbook. As beautiful as these Wyoming mountains were, they deserved a full spread in the story of her life.

They were a part of her now, just like the menagerie of animals who walked beside her.

Dad had been right. She'd never fit in when she'd lived in Buffalo Gap. But here, walking beside the man who held her heart, among people who were just like her, she finally felt like she was home.

TWELVE

Today had been hellish. It had been windy, which not only kicked Harrison's instincts up, but made it more dangerous to cut trees. Mason and Kirk were hard workers, but Mason was used to being behind a processor, Kirk was a sawmill worker, and neither had a ton of experience cutting trees on the side of a mountain. A deadly combination that kept Harrison instructing them more than getting his own work done.

They'd missed Damon's numbers, and by a lot, even though they'd all worked until sundown. Add to that, Clinton had been a bear on a rampage, and had Changed twice during the shift when they'd gotten into yelling arguments on the jobsite. And then he'd pitched a fit when Harrison had ordered him to come along for dinner at Moosey's Bait and

Barbecue. It was Audrey's first day of work, and he wanted them there to show support. She deserved to build a bond with shifters like them after all the lonely years. Plus, over the last few days, he'd noticed a massive change in her. She was joking and playing with the crew, opening up little by little. She even owned being a tiger shifter now, where she'd been utterly secretive about that part of her life when he'd first met her.

Oh, Harrison knew part of it was him. She was falling for him like he was for her, but he knew better than to take all the credit when the others were so clearly a part of her growing confidence.

"I still don't know why I had to come," Clinton groused from the front seat of Harrison's truck.

"Dude, just eat some barbecue and stop bitching," Kirk said from the back seat.

"I don't approve of what is happening, and it's horse crap that I'm forced to participate in all this kumbaya shit."

"Clinton, kindly shut the fuck up before I put my boot up your poop-chute," Bash muttered from the back seat.

Clinton turned in the passenger's seat and started punching at Bash, who was kicking up front with his big muddy work shoes.

Harrison slammed on the brakes in a parking spot outside of Moosey's and shoved Clinton hard against the window. He gripped his shirt, pinning him in place, and gritted out, "I'm beyond sick of your shit, man. You always hurt Audrey. You can see that, right? The way you treat her makes her smell sad and look sad, and she's been through enough rejection in her life. Do you seriously not care about someone who obviously cares about you? You know the beers that magically showed up in your fridge the other day? Her. You know the old barbecue grill that just happened to show up on your back porch? She spent four freaking hours refurbishing it. *For you*. Stop being an asshole." Harrison released his shirt and growled as Clinton immediately got out of the truck and slammed the door.

"C-team," Mason muttered, shaking his head as he got out.

Harrison scrubbed his hands over his face. He wanted to throw the damned truck into the woods just to work off some of his agitation. He'd known this wouldn't be easy, but he hadn't expected it to be this hard.

Maybe this was a bad idea. He didn't want to stress Audrey out more on her first day. She had an hour left on her shift, and he didn't want to ruin the end of the night by putting Clinton in her path.

He cut the engine and turned off the headlights, then followed the guys across the gravel parking lot.

Moosey's had started as a bait shop for the fishermen who traveled here from all over. Locals and tourists alike had made it thrive enough that Joey Dorsey, the owner, had added on a barbecue joint on the side that looked like an old, rustic garage. On warm days, like this one, Joey opened up the trio of doors that made up most of the front wall. From here, Harrison could see the busy interior. Most of the long picnic tables inside were taken, and half of the outside ones as well. Joey's meat man, Duncan, was standing in front of a massive grill, checking the temperature on a rack of ribs. Duncan waved a pair of tongs when he saw Harrison.

"Hey," he greeted him, forcing a smile. He was still pissed at Clinton, but Audrey wasn't just some human with dull senses. She would know immediately if he was angry, and he needed to get his growly bear under control.

He smelled her before he saw her. Mango shampoo, cherry lip gloss, and deliciously sexy fur. His crew was filing in through the open garage door to the left, but Harrison froze just on the edge of the parking lot. Audrey wore a tight black T-shirt with the bright pink Moosey's logo and short cut-offs that showed off her summer-tanned legs. She had her straight, dark hair pulled up high in the back of her head with a hairband, and she wore a smile on her lips as she wiped down an empty picnic table. Selfishly, he hoped she was thinking about him and that he was the cause of her happy expression.

Her nostrils flared slightly, and she turned to the crew who were making their way down the row toward her. All but Clinton who was now standing in line for food. Ass.

She hugged the boys one by one, and then looked around until her eyes locked on Harrison. The smile that had been so damned pretty a second ago turned boner-inducing. Fuck, his mate was gorgeous. His mate. He sighed as relief slid over his shoulders. Screw the bad day. She made everything better. Shoving his hands in his pockets, he gave her a smile and mouthed *hey*.

With an adorable self-conscious giggle, she smoothed her hand over her jean shorts and made her way around the table. "Hey," she said as soon as she was a few feet away. With a quick look at Duncan, who had his back turned, she lifted up on her tiptoes and gave Harrison a peck on the lips.

It wasn't enough though, so when she eased back, he chased her, angling his head and deepening the kiss. Every strand of tension that held his body so taut relaxed as hugged his neck and nibbled his bottom lip.

He let off a sigh of relief as she rubbed her cheek in cat-like affection against his. "How is your first day going?" he asked low.

She practically hummed with excitement. "Good. Everyone is so nice, the menu was super easy to learn, and this place stays busy so the day went by in a flash." She bumped his shoulder as he made his way inside where the crew was waiting in line. "I like this place a lot more than the diner I worked at. It's more laid back, and Joey introduced me to a lot of regulars today. How was your day?" she asked, fidgeting with the damp rag in her hands.

"Uh," Harrison murmured, glaring at Clinton. "It was a day. It's better now, though."

A frown marred her delicate, dark eyebrows, and his fingers itched to smooth it out. He didn't like her worrying when she'd looked so happy a second ago.

"We're going to talk about your rough day later, but right now, I'm going to take your order. I learned how to do that already. Meat and beer will make everything better." Audrey sauntered off toward the opening in the counter, hips swaying. "Hey," she said, turning with a happy grin. "I'm really glad you came to see me."

She didn't know it, but Audrey was the one who'd done him the favor. He'd been on the verge of an uncontrolled Change all day, but one look at his mate, and that pretty smile on her lips had turned his entire day around. God, he loved her, and soon, he was going to find the right time to tell her just how much. She deserved to hear how he really felt about her. She deserved to hear it every day because she was open with her feelings. She'd given him so much, and he'd been holding back, but as he watched her chatter happily with his crew as she took their orders, something struck him.

His life had lacked depth without her in it.

She was growing and gaining confidence, but he was changing, too.

He felt hope for his crew's future for the first time in a long time, and that was because of her. Because she looked at him like he was invincible and made him feel stronger than he had in years. She made him want to be a better alpha.

Clinton might not realize it yet, but Harrison did.

The Boarlanders needed her.

THIRTEEN

Today had been awesome! Audrey had a great first day working at Moosey's, had made thirty-two bucks from the tip jar on top of her hourly wage, and the Boarlanders had showed up at the end of the night like her very own personal, muscle-bound herd of cheerleaders.

They'd been hilarious and loud and had teased her mercilessly any time she worked close enough to their table, but she hadn't minded. If all the crew ignored her, like Clinton did, it would mean they didn't like her. But since they ribbed her like she was one of the guys, she took that as a sign of acceptance. And Harrison's eyes and easy smile had stayed pointed in her direction any time she'd glanced at him.

She'd never felt like this before—so happy and carefree. She'd never looked at her future and thought she could have it all—a man she loved more than anything, friends who understood her, and a chance at controlling the animal inside of her. Everything was falling into place for her in a way she'd never dreamt of.

Humming happily under her breath, Audrey peeled out of her Moosey's T-shirt and threw it in the washing machine. She had ordered enough differently colored work shirts to last a week, but until they came in, this one was all she had. In a rush, she pulled a red tank top on and made her way into the living room. She startled to a stop when a little, brown field mouse crossed the kitchen floor in front of her. He was dragging half a chocolate chip cookie, as well as a humongous set of testicles.

"You must be Nards," she murmured as she waited patiently for him to amble out of her way.

With a shake of her head at the strange turn her life had taken, she made her way across the squishy flooring. The second she hit the night air, she inhaled deeply. The air was so clean and crisp here, and the moon above was full and a gorgeous orange color. Feeling like a million bucks, she jogged down the stairs and headed for Harrison's trailer at the opposite end of the park.

Mason was replacing the decking of his stairs with the leftover lumber from 1010's newly built porch, and he waved to her as she strode by. "If you're looking for your man, he left a few minutes ago."

Audrey frowned at Harrison's parked truck in front of his trailer. "Where did he go?"

"Checking the border probably. He headed off through there." Mason pointed across the road to a trail that led between Kirk and Bash's trailers and off into the woods.

"Thanks, Mason."

Audrey altered her route and grinned as an idea struck her. Harrison had said she should let her tiger out more often, and in her downtime between the lunch and dinner rush today, she'd thought about her Change last night. What if he was right? What if someday, with enough practice, she could have instant, painless Changes like Harrison and the others? She knew one thing. She sure as hell didn't want a repeat of last night when her mate watched her suffer through a Change.

She could surprise him with her tiger and let him see how hard she was trying. He would be proud of her, just like he had been last night. Plus, she would be able to find him easier out in the woods as a big cat. She had whiskers to feel vibration, better eyesight, ears made for hearing everything, and big, flat paws to stalk quietly. She could sneak up on him if she was brave enough to Change again.

She could find her courage for Harrison.

The strange, orange moon cast an ethereal glow over the Boarlander woods, dappling the forest floor in soft shadow and light. At the edge of a small meadow, a speckle illuminated the dark in the distance, and then another shone closer. When she walked to the center of the meadow, brushing her hands over the hip-high wild grass, hundreds of fireflies lifted up from their shelter.

Her breath caught in her throat at how beautiful this place was with the lightning bugs blinking constantly like holiday lights. Surrounded by such beauty, this was the perfect spot for her to ask her tiger to come out. She was nervous, sure, and her hands shook badly, but if Audrey needed to endure such pain, maybe it would be easier if she was staring at something so breathtaking. Winking bugs, winking stars, and the orange man on the moon. She wouldn't be alone.

Her breath trembled now as she shucked

her shorts and peeled her shirt over her head. Audrey folded them neatly into a pile and set her sneakers on top.

With a long, steadying breath, she lay down and stared at the night sky one last time. Closing her eyes, she imagined her body as a tiger's and asked her animal for the honor of her form. A soft satisfied purr sounded from her throat, and then pain blasted up her nerve endings. Audrey seized and grunted at the agony, but focused on counting.

One, two...

Her bones broke through.

Three, four...

No purring anymore.

Five, six...

Too much pain to fix.

Seven, eight...

Too late.

Nine, ten...

She didn't want to go back again.

With a proud feline smile, Audrey pushed up onto all fours as the last of her fur prickled her skin, covering her body and shielding her from the cool breeze.

She looked over her shoulder at her long, lithe body. White fur with thin black stripes, she was bigger than any tiger she'd seen in a zoo. Her tail twitched, and she panted slightly from the effort of the Change, but now she could smell him—her mate.

And she could hear him, too.

This was the upside to the monster...no, not the monster. This was the upside to her animal. She wasn't a monster. She never had been. Just different, and out here, different was good. It was coveted and important.

Harrison, Harrison, Harrison. Strong, handsome, caring mate, always putting his crew in front of himself. He could've grown up a brute, just like his dad, but he had been stronger than that. Someday, he would make a good father to their cubs. Tigers or bears, it didn't matter what animals her children would harbor. She would raise them to be proud of their feral sides, like she was now proud of hers. The purr was back in her throat. *Happy kitty.*

She wove through the blinking meadow, and Harrison's voice got louder. Excited by the thought of seeing him, she loped faster, head up, ears erect. Hunting for her mate, hunting for cuddles.

"That was your idea," another voice said. Clinton.

Confused, Audrey slowed, hesitated, then

stalked silently forward. She could see them now in the distance.

Cicadas sang in waves, frogs croaked, and above, a family of birds chattered quietly. Little rustlings sounded from burrows and hidey holes in the forest floor. So many little heartbeats, but the biggest, most important one belonged to Harrison.

Facing the river, he stood with his back to her. A waterfall splashed down into the pool in front of him and Clinton. Her mate had showed her this place last night. Bear Trap Falls. Harrison's jeans clung to his powerful, splayed legs. His shoulders were wide and flexed against his cotton shirt as he shoved his hands into his pockets and shook his head. A soft growl sounded from him. He wasn't happy. Audrey narrowed her eyes at Clinton. He was the source of most unhappiness around here. She should bite him.

She hunched down, bunching her muscles for an attack, but he turned to Harrison. His face wasn't the mask of fury that he usually wore around her. He looked...sad. She froze.

"The day I came to you, begging for you to take me into your crew, you said no ladies allowed at the park. To me, that's what made it worth leaving the Gray Backs. I loved them.

They were home, but my bear couldn't handle what was happening there. You said all potential claims for any of your crew had to be run by you first, and then you said you would give us the same courtesy. We had a say in any of your potential claims."

"Clinton—"

"No, let me say my piece. I checked every crew I can think of, and there are no bachelor groups left. And I won't make it long as a rogue bear. My animal will go mad fast, and no one will be there to put me down."

"Clinton, you're going mad now!"

"And I want you to be the one to put me down when the time comes, Harrison."

"Fuck," Harrison growled out, linking his hands behind his head.

"But for now, I have nowhere else to go. I've looked. This place is it. This is my last stand."

"That's a copout. You aren't even trying."

"You're wrong."

"So, what do you want me to do? I'm trying to move us forward, but you're trying to keep us in the hole, man."

"I don't want you to claim Audrey."

Harrison jerked his gaze to Clinton, and the smell of fury wafted to her on the breeze.

"Please tell me you're joking."

Clinton shook his head for a long time, gaze on the babbling river under the falls. "Don't bring her in any closer."

"For how long?"

"For always. I don't want her to be a Boarlander. I know what I can and can't handle right now, and that's it. The second you give her a claiming mark, this place is wide open to females, and my bear can't be around couples, Harrison." Clinton arched his eyebrows, and his voice broke on the quiet "I'm sorry" he murmured before he turned and walked through the trees toward the trailer park.

Shocked, Audrey watched him disappear into the trees. It was impossible to breathe under the weight of the pain that filled her chest. She would never be a Boarlander, would never be Harrison's claim. She would be destined to stay on the outside here, never really a part of this place, just like the rest of her life had been.

She dragged her horrified gaze to Harrison, but he didn't smell like fury anymore. The air was heavy with his sadness.

The word "Fuck!" echoed across Bear Trap Falls as he squatted down, hands gripping the back of his neck. He looked as hurt in his middle as she was. Gut punched. She wanted to retch.

She wished she could be angry with Clinton, but now she understood him. He wasn't being mean because he hated her like she'd thought. There was something wrong with his bear. Something broken, and someday, Harrison would have to put him down.

Clinton wasn't asking for her to be cast aside to hurt her.

He was pushing her out so he could live longer.

Why did she feel like the earth had just opened up and swallowed her whole? Why did she feel like she'd just been trapped in a dark cave alone? Harrison, her mate, was out of reach. If she begged him to claim her and bring her into the Boarlanders, he would hurt. If she didn't, he would hurt. His crew was everything to him, and she was causing a huge rift in the make-up.

She'd been selfish in moving into 1010, knowing that not all of Harrison's crew was okay with her living here. It had been easy to ignore the sadness and anger that Clinton let off because she'd had Harrison. He was the sun blocking out the dark, but with Clinton's admission here in these woods, she couldn't ignore the grit she'd caused anymore.

She loved Harrison.

Loved him.

And now she would have to let him go.

FOURTEEN

A knock sounded at the front door of 1010. Audrey was already distancing herself from thinking of it as *home* anymore.

She stood from the edge of the bed where she'd been lost in thought and wringing her hands for the past half an hour.

Maybe she shouldn't answer it.

Another knock echoed through the trailer. She would've feigned sleep, but the bedroom light was on, so she wouldn't be tricking anyone.

With a quick trio of huffed breaths, she pulled open the door. Harrison stood on the porch he'd built for her, his back to her, hands on his hips. He turned, and the devastated look in his lightened eyes made her duck her gaze. She couldn't take anymore hurt right now.

"You were out there. I smelled your fur in

the woods on my way back. What did you hear?"

"Everything," she whispered. She ghosted a glance up to him and then back to his scuffed boots.

"Can I come in?" he asked.

Stepping back, Audrey opened the door wider. Harrison kissed her cheek as he passed, and she squeezed her eyes closed so she wouldn't cry. Sweet mate, worried about her, making sure she knew she was still adored.

"We should talk about what Clinton asked."

"Will you claim me against his wishes?"

Harrison ran his hands roughly over his hair and wouldn't meet her eyes, which was answer enough.

"Then I don't want to talk about it. I just want you to hold me until I fall asleep." *One last time.*

Harrison froze, his ice-blue eyes locked on her. "Okay," he murmured. He squeezed her hand and led her slowly to the bedroom.

Beside the bed, he pulled her clothes off gently, piece by piece, then tucked her under the covers. He turned off the light, and as her eyes adjusted to the dark, the rustle of fabric sounded. The covers lifted, letting in the cool window breeze, and then Harrison slipped in beside her.

He was so warm and strong, muscles hard against her back as he spooned her, and that beautiful, all-consuming feeling of safety washed over her. She closed her eyes just to drink in this moment fully.

His cheek resting on hers, Harrison whispered, "Everything will be okay. You'll see. I'll fix it."

But fixing it would require him to hurt his crew, and she couldn't have that. Not anymore. The Boarlanders felt like her crew, too, even if it wasn't true. Hurting one of them continually would wreck her. She and Harrison would both go down in flames, so she had to be strong now. She had to save them both.

He dipped his lips to her neck and kissed her gently, and she responded by arching her back against him in a silent plea. *Erase my thoughts for a little while. Let me pretend this was meant to last forever.*

Harrison gripped her waist and rocked his hips backward. When he pushed forward, his thick erection rested between her thighs. Good mate. With a sigh, she let go of everything and reached over her shoulder, gripped the back of his neck as he slid his shaft slowly into her.

He didn't rush, didn't lose control. Instead, he moved smoothly in and out, then in again with a graceful roll of his hips. His stomach flexed against her back with the pace he set. Sexy, powerful mate. His arms slid around her stomach, and she moaned. They fit together so well—perfectly. His hand brushed down her stomach and cupped her sex as she rolled her hips with the pace he set.

This right here could never be mistaken for fucking. Harrison was making love to her. He was making up for what she'd heard in the woods. He was trying to fuse the break in her heart, and for that, she adored him even more.

But usually, he tempted himself with grazing his teeth against the oversensitive skin on her back, but tonight, all he did was lay a single, soft kiss right where he couldn't claim her. No teeth, no teasing. It was a silent request that a kiss there be enough. That she be okay with being an outsider. A rogue, as Clinton had called it. That was what she had been, and that's what she would always be.

Harrison's grip tightened as he moved within her faster, and he rasped out her name. The pressure built slowly, and her body pulsed around his cock the instant he went ridged against her back and spilled the first shot of his warmth into her. His lips plucked at her neck as he bucked, emptying himself, and her aftershocks pounded on.

As he relaxed against her, she dragged his hand from her stomach to her lips and kissed his knuckles. Snuggling his palm against her cheek, she blinked a single tear from the corner of her eye. She would hold onto this moment forever. She would commit it to memory because it would have to be enough.

She was a lucky one. Some people never found this depth of emotion, and she'd held a worthy man's heart in her hands for a blinding moment in time.

"I love you, Audrey," Harrison murmured.

Her face crumpled in the dark, and she swallowed her heartbreak.

When she was able, she whispered, "I love you, too."

FIFTEEN

An echoing bang sounded down the side of the trailer, and Harrison lurched up in bed. Completely disoriented, he frowned at the unfamiliar room, then down at Audrey, who lay undisturbed beside him.

"Five more minutes," she murmured in a sleepy voice.

The gray morning light that filtered through the windows on either side of the headboard cast soft shadows against her cheeks. Her dark hair was fanned across the pillow, shining like silk, and her long lashes rested on her lightly freckled cheeks. She looked like an angel come to earth.

The banging sounded again, this time at the front door.

"Boss Bear, you in there?" Bash asked. "It's time to get ready for work."

Startled, Harrison jerked his gaze to the clock on the night stand. *6:00 am.*

What the hell? He'd slept through the night.

Audrey stretched and let off an adorable sleep sound as she reached for him. Harrison ran his hand over his facial scruff and tried to wrap his head around what she'd done. He hadn't slept through the night since he was a kid. It hadn't been physically possible, but Audrey had done something unexpected to him. He'd always thought a mate would make him more restless at night with his heightened senses to protect her, but Audrey had done the opposite. She'd made him feel safe enough to sleep beside her. No middle-of-the-night patrols or moving around the trailer checking the locks on the doors. No getting up at every noise to make sure all was well in the trailer park.

Just…sleep.

The smile that stretched his face felt good.

"Boss Bear!"

"Yeah, all right," Harrison muttered as he slipped out from under Audrey's arm and padded to the front door. Bare-ass naked, he cracked the door open, squinting against the dawn light. "I'll be right out."

Bash looked troubled, though, and usually he was a morning person.

"What's wrong?"

"Clinton knows you spent the night here." Bash shifted his weight uncomfortably. "He's challenged me for Second. The official kind of fight."

"Shit. When?"

"Right now. He wants more say in what goes on. Boss, he's gonna dig his heels in."

"He already has. Go get ready. I'll be right there."

"Oh," Bash murmured, turning at the porch stairs. "Boarlanders only. Clinton already told Kirk and Mason to stay inside until it's done. We don't need anyone else throwing in an extra challenge for rank." He lifted his dark eyebrows and gave Harrison a significant look before he jogged down the stairs and back toward his trailer.

Great. Clinton could win this. Bash was a brawler, and when he and Clinton fought unofficially, they were neck and neck. But Clinton was working on desperation and had been feeding off anger this whole week. An unstable Clinton becoming Second right now could cripple the Boarlanders even more. Fuckety-fucksticks.

When Harrison went back into Audrey's bedroom, she smiled in her sleep but didn't stir so, as quietly as he could, he dressed. The fight would be over in a matter of minutes, and from the sound of her deep breathing, she would sleep right through it, which was perfect. He didn't want to hurt her worse with the explanation of why she couldn't watch. She wasn't a Boarlander, and if Clinton had his way, she never would be.

He didn't know how he was going to solve that little dilemma yet, but he would figure something out because Audrey was his. His mate, his love, his happiness, the future mother of his cubs—she was everything.

He kissed her hair lightly and made his way out of 1010. With a lengthened gait, he strode for his trailer to get ready fast. Clinton was already stretching his neck out near the park sign beside Harrison's trailer.

"Thanks for ignoring what I said last night, prick," Clinton said through a sneer.

"I spent the night with her. Didn't claim her." Harrison jogged up his stairs and slammed the door behind him, barely able to contain the urge to Change and rip Clinton limb from limb. Last night, Clinton had seemed lucid in his request, but this morning he was the conductor of the Asshole Express again, and Harrison was really tired of being told how to run his crew.

One of these days, Clinton would push too hard and get booted from the Boarlanders, consequences be damned. A fact which Clinton probably realized. Why else would he be in such a rush to establish himself in the pecking order here?

Clinton was a clever monster, even with a messed up bear, and he was playing a game of chess Harrison hadn't realized before now. Clinton had been slowly moving everyone into place until he got the exact dysfunctional crew he wanted, and last night had been the last straw. He'd asked too much, and demanded Harrison walk too fine a line.

Clinton had hurt Audrey with his request. Oh, Harrison had heard her crying after they'd had sex, and that wasn't on him. That was on Clinton and his messed-up bear's inability to adapt to change.

Never let her be a Boarlander? He couldn't even wrap his mind around that. She belonged here as surely as any of them did. Harrison didn't have a solution to keeping Audrey and Clinton both happy, but damn it all, he was going to find one. All he needed was time.

He took a two minute shower, brushed his teeth, and dressed for his shift, then grabbed his hurriedly packed sack lunch off the counter and snatched his hard hat from beside the door before he left. He tossed his stuff into the passenger's seat of his truck, then jogged over to where Bash and Clinton were waiting.

Both smelled like fur and fury, and matching snarls rattled their chests as they circled each other.

"Keep it clean," Harrison instructed. "Don't kill each other. Just establish dominance, and let's move on. If you keep fighting after one of you gives in, I *will* intervene and rip you a new asshole, understood?"

"Yeah, boss," Bash growled out.

Clinton spat in the dirt. "Fine."

"Harrison?" Audrey asked from behind.

Shee-yit. He turned, hand out to stop her progress. "Stop there."

"Are you fucking kidding me?" Clinton snarled. "Boarlanders only!"

Harrison stifled a growl and jammed a finger at Clinton. "Shut up, man. She didn't know."

"What's happening?" she asked, confusion pooling in her soft brown eyes.

"A battle for Second that you weren't

invited to," Clinton yelled.

"Boss said stop talking to her like that!" Bash hunched, and his dark grizzly burst from him. He roared at Clinton, his breath steaming in the cool morning air. He landed on all fours so hard the ground vibrated.

"Audrey, get back inside," Harrison said. "Use my trailer."

Hurt slashed across her face. "No girls allowed again?"

"No!" Clinton barked. "No outsiders allowed! Now scamper inside before I challenge your mate for his rank, too, 'cause I have to tell you, I'm mighty fuckin' tempted right now."

"Clinton, enough!" Harrison roared from behind where Bash paced, waiting for Clinton to Change.

"At least I would uphold the damned rules!" Clinton exclaimed, his face going red. He smelled off. Crazy. Unbalanced. Sick.

"Audrey, run!" Harrison bellowed, bolting for her. He had to keep her safe, had to protect her from Clinton's wrath, because as his massive, blond grizzly burst from his skin, his murderous eyes weren't on Bash anymore. They were on…him.

Clinton was charging him. Fuck. He forced

a Change, pushed it as fast as he could, but Clinton was on him. He got a claw across Harrison's ribcage, but then with a loud *oomf*, Clinton was thrown sideways.

With a shake of his head, Harrison winced and stood on all fours, ready to finish this. But Clinton wasn't after him anymore. No, now that big yellow-haired bear was on the defense from one snarling, hissing, clawing, pissed-off tigress.

Audrey disengaged and stood sideways as Clinton stumbled back a few paces. His shoulder was bleeding freely, and red was staining Audrey's side, but she didn't favor it as she hissed and charged, her graceful body a weapon as she leapt on Clinton's back and went to town on his neck. Clinton spun and dislodged her, and the fight meshed into a blur of violence.

He had to stop this.

"No," Bash said, standing in front of him. "Let her do this."

Harrison looked at him in horror. She was a tiger, much smaller than Clinton's bear. Sure, she was fast as the crack of a whip and holding her own, but she wasn't ready for this. Was she?

The sound of Audrey and Clinton's

enraged battle roars shook the entire damned trailer park, and Harrison stood frozen as Audrey controlled the fight, pushing Clinton farther and farther away. He huffed a shocked sound as he realized what his mate was doing. She was battling for him. She was pushing Clinton's rage as far away from Harrison as she could, and taking teeth and claws to do it.

Holy shit, she was beautiful. This whole time, her entire life, Audrey had been hiding a badass brawler beast inside of her.

Clinton went down hard and froze on the ground. Smart grizzly because Audrey's long teeth were clamped on his neck. One twitch of her head and she could end him.

In a rush, Harrison shrank back to his human form and called out, "Audrey, don't! It's over now. Let him up."

She hesitated for a terrifying moment, then released him and slunk gracefully back toward Harrison, placing herself between him and Clinton. Brave, protective mate.

Clinton dragged his maimed body upward until all four paws were splayed on the ground. His fur was striping with wet crimson, and he swayed on his feet.

"I retract my challenge for Second," Bash said, crossing his arms over his bare chest as he leveled Harrison with a steady, bright-eyed look. "Call it."

Rocked to his core, Harrison dragged his gaze from Clinton to the white tiger with her lips curled back in a hiss, exposing long, razor sharp canines that dripped red.

Beaston had been right. She'd bled Clinton.

Softly, Harrison murmured, "Audrey takes Second."

SIXTEEN

Second? She wasn't even a Boarlander, and that wasn't what she'd meant to do at all. She'd only meant to protect Harrison from Clinton's unexpected attack.

She'd seen Clinton's eyes as he'd charged Harrison, who had his focus on her and getting her to safety, instead of Changing to defend himself. It was so messed up that Clinton would charge his alpha while he was in human form. Her fury had spurred on a quick Change the second she'd decided to protect Harrison. He'd been attacked like that before by his dad, and she would be good-goddamned if she was going to stand by and watch that happen again.

Clinton shrank into his human skin with a grunt of pain, and Audrey winced at what she'd done to him. She'd never let loose like that before, but he'd hurt her, too. The sting of claw marks and puncture wounds zinged up her nerve endings, and her ribcage was too warm, too wet.

"What have you done?" he asked her through gritted teeth. Clinton turned and limped toward his trailer.

"Clinton!" Harrison barked out.

"I'm leaving!" Clinton yelled over his shoulder. "I should've left the minute she came around, but I didn't. I gave you a chance to fix this, and now she's our damned Second? Hell no."

Leave? Clinton couldn't leave. Already, Harrison was cursing under his breath, bent over, arms locked on his knees like he was being gutted.

Audrey bolted after Clinton. When Mason came out of his trailer and stood in her way, she snarled. He lifted his hands in surrender and backed out of the way. Good pig.

Kirk sat on top of Mason's trailer in his gorilla form, tension oozing from him, eyes zeroed in on Clinton as the injured idiot made his way into the next singlewide.

"Audrey, let him be," Bash said half-heartedly from behind. Maybe if Harrison had given the order, she would have to obey him, she didn't know, but Bash was easy to ignore. She wasn't hunting Clinton. She was trying to help him.

She skidded to a stop, her wide paws going flat against the gravel as she slid. Heaving breath, she closed her eyes and Changed back. It wasn't instant, or even quick. In fact, it took too damned long and felt like she'd injected every cell of her body with gasoline and lit a match, but she had to fix this.

With a sob of pain, she stumbled upward and sagged against the splintered railing of Clinton's porch. Her body hurt, and not just from the Change. She was healing some massive claw marks on her side, and as she forced her legs up the stairs, wetness dripped down her hip. Clinton had left a blood trail. She'd hurt him. She gagged and steadied herself on the door handle, then shoved the door open.

"Clinton?" she called in a hoarse voice.

"Fuck off, *Second*." His pissed-off snarl came from the bedroom on the other side of the kitchen, so she padded unsteadily in there. At the open doorway, she halted. Clinton was packing a duffle bag.

"You can't leave."

"Well, I sure as shit can't stay!"

"Clinton, this isn't what I want! I didn't even know I was fighting for Second. I was just trying to keep you off Harrison until he could Change. Until it would be fair."

"Yeah, I know." Clinton gritted his teeth and clamped his hands onto the unmade bedspread, clutching the comforter in his fists. "I shouldn't have attacked him." He dragged his bright gaze to her. "I'm not okay with you around. I can't do this."

"Please don't run."

"Don't you know? That's what I do. Crew to crew."

"And where does it stop? When do you decide this is it for you? That it's enough? Clinton, you'll hurt Harrison if you go. He's put up with all your shit, with you pushing his damned crew away, and he did that for you. So he could keep you."

"Audrey?" Bash asked from the front room.

"No!" She and Clinton both yelled.

"Okay," Bash said in a small voice, then slammed the door behind him.

"Look," Clinton said, looking sick. "It's not you. It's me."

"And where will you go?"

Clinton shook his head for a long time, then began to pack again.

She was shaking from the adrenaline dump in her system, leaking red onto his laminate flooring and naked as the day she was born, but none of that mattered. She couldn't be the cause of the Boarlanders shattering.

"I'm leaving," she murmured. "I decided to last night when I heard you ask Harrison not to claim me. Out by the river. My mind is already made up."

"But Harrison—"

"Will be hurt if you go. He's not bound to me. Not yet. You pledged to him, though, and he's been through hell losing his crew." She turned for the door but hesitated at the frame. "Just...promise me you'll try harder. Promise me you'll take care of him."

"Audrey, you can't go now. You're Second. You earned a place here."

She smiled sadly. "I was always on the outside, Clinton. I'm used to it. You need Harrison and this place. I'll mend over time, but you won't." Lies. She would never be okay again.

She would not expose her heartbreak to Clinton, so she patted the doorframe and left his trailer, tears stinging her eyes. She couldn't draw a deep enough breath as she made her way to 1010.

Harrison sat on the top porch stair, elbows on his knees, favoring a long claw mark across his ribs. They matched. She would always think about that if her injuries made scars. Every time she saw them in her reflection, she would remember how she'd gotten them, fighting for the man she loved. For the man she would always love. Down to her marrow, she knew Harrison was it for her. No one else for the rest of her life would compare.

Harrison watched her approach and stood when she got closer.

"Clinton's not leaving," she said, climbing the stairs.

"He's not?" There was beautiful hope in his voice, and she barely resisted the urge to double over the pain in her middle.

"No. I am."

"Wait, what?" Harrison followed her inside.

"I'm not a part of this place. Never was, never will be without the crew's blessing, and I can't get that from Clinton." She strode into the bedroom and yanked her suitcase from the closet. "You can't claim me with Clinton here, and I won't be the reason he leaves. One of us has to go."

"Audrey, you can't go now. I'm yours. My bear...fuck. Stop!" He yanked the suitcase from her hand, but she began stacking her clothes from the drawers to the bed without missing a beat.

She needed to do this as fast as possible, or she would lose her courage.

"I need you to stay," he said, low and growly. "I need you to pick me back."

"I am." She stomped her foot and dashed her knuckles over the tears streaming down her cheeks. "Can't you see I am? It's me or Clinton, Harrison. He was here first."

She dressed quickly as he watched her from his spot, leaned up against the wall. She didn't dare a look directly at him, or she would buckle. She picked up the suitcase Harrison had dropped on the floor and packed it as fast as she could.

She was trying so hard to be strong, but her vision was completely hindered by the tears that rimmed her eyes, and she couldn't breathe through the sobs that clawed their way up the back of her throat.

When she passed Harrison, he pulled gently on her wrist. Closing her eyes, she shook her head in despair. Harrison pulled her gently toward him, and she was helpless to deny him. She wanted him to hold her. She wanted to pretend it could've been like this forever.

"I can't make you stay, can I?" he asked, his face buried against her neck.

Unable to speak, she shook her head.

"If I make this place good for you someday, will you come back?"

This was her future disappearing like fog under the bright sun. As long as Harrison was the strong, caring alpha he was, he would try to rehabilitate Clinton. It was part of why she loved him. The only way she would be able to come back was if Clinton was gone, and she would never wish for such a thing.

Instead of answering, she whispered, "I love you, Harrison. I always will." She pushed up on her tiptoes and kissed him, then ripped herself away and left 1010. Left the happy life she'd finally found, the friends who made her feel whole.

And as she drove away, she saw him in her rearview. Harrison's bear strode for the woods with long, powerful strides. Just before he hit the tree line, he looked at her and roared a heartbreaking sound.

She would never be the same again, would never be okay.

Darkness had been easy to dwell in before she'd known the light.

Now and for always, it would be impossible to be happy in the shadows again.

SEVENTEEN

Audrey was dying. That was the only thing that could explain this gutted, hollow feeling that had her doubled over the steering wheel of her Jeep, shaking with the pain.

The gravel road curved this way and that like some great serpent through the mountains. Ancient evergreens lined the road, and each turn brought a new breathtaking view of Damon's mountains. She would never see this place again.

She maneuvered a sharp switchback and gasped when she saw Clinton standing in the middle of the road. She slammed on her brakes and skidded to a dusty stop right before she hit him.

When the dirt cloud cleared, he was pacing up the road, then back, eyes panicked. His blond hair was spiked up like he'd been running his hands through it, and he was heaving breath as though he'd rushed over a great distance. His gray eyes were bright, but not with panic or the inhuman side of him. He just looked…scared.

Audrey rolled down the window. "Are you okay?"

"Turn off the engine!"

Okaaay. Audrey put it in park and cut the engine.

"I can't do this if you can just leave, or drive around me, or…get out. Please, Audrey, get out so I can think."

Audrey wiped her eyes on the sleeve of her shirt and kicked open the door, then got out gingerly.

"I hurt you, I hurt Harrison, and I hurt the Boarlanders. I was so shoved up my own ass with my problems, I couldn't see that until now." He paced away again, scrubbing his hands down his jaw.

"I don't understand."

"No, no. You understood everything. I didn't." Clinton sat heavily on a boulder on the side of the road and buried his head in his hands. "Just wait so I can figure this out. It's too fast, and now it feels wrong that you're leaving. This whole time it's all I wanted, but…" He stared at her, shaking his head back and forth like he couldn't believe what had unfolded. "I don't know if it's because you're Second or if it was that awful sound from Harrison's throat when you drove away, but I'm not okay with you leaving."

"Well, I'm not okay with *you* leaving!" she barked out. "And I don't want to play this game. The who-deserves-to-be-here-most game. It hurts, Clinton. It hurts me, it hurts Harrison, and deep down, I think it hurts you, too. You won! You pushed everyone away, pushed most of Harrison's bears out of the park, and now you've pushed me away from the only man who has ever really understood me."

"I didn't want that. I couldn't remember—"
"Clinton—"
"I couldn't remember how it was! I had that. What you and Harrison have, I've been there."

"What?"

"I've had people and lost them, and it's my fault they aren't here with me anymore, Audrey. I'm cursed, and in my own fucked-up way, I was trying to protect you, Harrison, Bash, and most of all…" He swallowed hard. "Most of all, I was trying to forget how great being paired up can be."

"Oh God, Clinton." She sat on the rock next to him, shoulder to shoulder, overlooking a pine valley. She stared at the sunrise and sighed. "I'm sorry about your loss, but you can't run from *feeling*. You'll hurt the people around you even worse than you're hurting yourself."

"Yeah, I figured that out. You just came in and shook everything up, you know? I'd finally got to a point where I felt okay, and then you came along and Harrison wanted to turn the park upside down."

"No, Harrison wanted that before I came along. He wants to make a good crew, Clinton. Where you are right now isn't where a good alpha would want you to be. Harrison isn't using change as a weapon. He's using it as a cast to fix what's been broken until you can stand on your own again."

Clinton huffed a laugh and picked up a stick from the ground, then broke it in half. "Come back," he said in a barely audible voice.

"What?"

"You heard me." Clinton shot her a glance, then broke the stick in his hands again. "Come back and help him become the alpha he's meant to be."

"And what about you?"

"I won't run. I'll stay. I'll try. Just…come back. I don't want Harrison cut off at the legs because of something I've forced. I've got enough guilt to shoulder without an annoying…admittedly badass…tiger shifter added to the pile."

"I did kick your stumpy tail."

Clinton snorted. "It was a close fight, and I was taken off guard. At least, that's what I'm going to tell the Gray Backs." He chucked the broken stick over the side of the road. "Willa's going to lose her shit when she hears the Boarlander Second is another lady shifter."

"I don't know anything about being a Second, and I'm not even pledged to this crew, so any time you want to challenge for it, just say the word," she muttered, squinting against the rising sunlight.

"Nah, I think I'm gonna let this one ride. I'm not okay, and it'll hurt the crew if I climb the ranks right now. Come on." Clinton stood and dusted the seat of his pants, then offered his hand to help her up.

She narrowed her eyes at him. "Is this the part where you push me over the side of the cliff and drive my Jeep into a lake somewhere?"

Clinton gave a tired sigh. "Don't tempt me, tiger-lady."

Cautiously, she slid her palm against his, but he only helped her up and then jogged to her Jeep. "I'll drive. I can get you to Harrison faster."

"Okay," she murmured, utterly astonished at the turn her life had suddenly taken.

Was this real? Could she keep this life she'd found, nestled in the heart of Damon's mountains with people who actually understood her? Could she keep the man she loved?

Cautiously, she opened the passenger side door as the ignition roared to life. "Clinton, if this is some kind of trick—"

"It's not," he said, and there it was again. That honest note she was learning to decipher.

Heart thumping double-time in her chest, she climbed in and buckled up. Safety first and all, and definitely *not* because Clinton could still drive them over a cliff at a whim.

He'd been right about getting her to Harrison sooner. Why? Because he drove like a bear out of hell and barely even slowed for the steep switchbacks. Eventually, she closed her eyes, grabbed the oh-shit bar, and hoped she survived long enough to see her man again.

Clinton pulled under the Boarland Mobile Park sign and skidded to a stop in front of Mason and Kirk, who sat in some broken-down plastic lawn chairs with matching frowns.

The second she was free of the door, she asked, "Where is he?"

"Oh, thank God," Mason said, leaning back in his chair. "He's in the woods. Bash went after him."

She bolted for the trail between Kirk and Bash's trailer.

"Audrey!" Kirk called.

"Yeah?" she yelled over her shoulder.

"It's real good to have you back, Second."

Skidding to a stop, she grinned at the three men who'd become so unexpectedly important to her. Cupping her hands around her mouth, she called, "It feels ridiculously good to be back."

She ran for the woods, following Harrison's well-worn trail he'd made by checking the Boarlander border countless times in the years he'd lived here. She didn't know how she knew, but he was at Bear Trap Falls. She could feel him, like a rope tied from her heart to his. The pain in her chest eased with every step she took toward him.

The sound of the falls was music to her ears as she pushed her legs faster and faster through the forest. And when the riverbank came into view, she slowed and then stopped at what she saw. Harrison was knelt at the edge of the gently lapping waves, his hands linked behind his head, while Bash crouched beside him, murmuring something too low for her to hear.

The air was stifling, and the scent of pain, of sadness, overwhelmed her. "Harrison," she whispered.

Bash jerked his gaze to her and froze beside his alpha. Feature by feature, his face relaxed, and a slow smile spread his lips. Beside him, Harrison stood. His shoulders lifted with his ragged breath, and slowly, he turned a wild gaze on her. His eyes were the color of snow, but that didn't scare her. He was the most beautiful thing she'd ever seen.

She walked, then jogged, then ran to him. He seemed shocked and barely got his arms up fast enough to catch her. Audrey was crying now, unable to contain her happiness as his hands slid gently up her back.

"Audrey?" he asked in a broken voice.

"Clinton said I can stay. We're both

staying." She eased back and cupped his cheeks. "Harrison, I choose you."

His chest heaved as he searched her eyes. He looked at Bash, then back at her and asked in a hoarse voice, "You talked to Clinton?"

"Yes, yes. He stopped me from leaving and asked me to stay. No more running, from Clinton or from me. You can keep us both. You can keep me." Her voice faded to nothing as emotion tightened her throat.

"It's true," Clinton said from the woods where he approached Bear Trap Falls, flanked by Kirk and Mason. "A wise alpha once told me she would be good for the Boarlanders." Clinton gave a slight smile. "And I trust him."

"She will be," Harrison said through a growing smile. "You'll see." He leaned down and kissed her.

She squeaked as Bash lifted them both up in a back-cracking hug. Her organs were on the verge of popping like water balloons, but she couldn't find it in her to care as Bash's booming laugh echoed through the woods.

And as she looked from Harrison's adoring gaze to Bash's megawatt grin to Clinton, leaning against a tree with a sad smile on his face, to Kirk with his arm thrown over Mason's shoulder, she took stock of this moment. It was one of those life-changing ones—the end of something hard and the beginning of something great.

She was here for the beginning of the new Boarlanders, and she was going to have a front row seat watching her mate make them into the best fucking crew in Damon's mountains.

EPILOGUE

Audrey hung the painting Willa had made her on the nail she'd hammered into the wall in 1010's living room. It still made her giggle every time she looked at the terrible picture of her and Harrison's animals holding hands, frolicking under a rainbow in a patch of grass, flowers, and worms. Anything that made her this happy should be hung where she could see it every day.

In the last month, she'd found more happiness than she knew what to do with. Joey Dorsey had given her a raise and more hours at work, she was getting to know the regulars who came in for barbecue and bait, and she was making deep, meaningful friendships with the Gray Backs and Ashe Crew. She'd carved out a place among this rag-tag crew, and somewhere along the way, even Clinton had accepted her presence here. And little by little, the Boarlanders were working to clean up the trailer park. But most importantly, she'd fallen even deeper in love with Harrison. He didn't patrol as much at night anymore, and when he did, Audrey Changed with him and walked the Boarlander woods beside her mate, making sure her life here, and her friends, were safe.

A knock sounded on her door, and she straightened the painting before she answered it.

Harrison grinned down at her with that easy smile he always had ready. "I have a surprise for you."

"*We* have a surprise for you," Bash called from the newly mowed weeds in the front yard.

She waved at Bash, Clinton, Kirk, and Mason. "What's going on?"

"Come on, kitty," Harrison said, offering his hand.

Baffled, she smiled at them before shoving her feet into a pair of flip-flops and followed Harrison across the porch and down the stairs where Bash pulled her scrapbook from behind his back.

"Oh, my gosh, you guys are not supposed to see this!" She yanked it away and clutched it to her chest as her cheeks blazed with embarrassment. Showing Harrison her secret self had been one thing, but the rest of them? Nope, nope, nope.

"Your cheeks are the color of cherries," Bash said. Remorseless oaf.

"Don't freak out. Just look at the modifications we did," Harrison murmured.

Her mortification was bottomless, but at their goading, her curiosity won out. Carefully, she opened to the cover page. Her homemade house cat with the glued-on black stripes was gone, and in its place was a white tiger with bloody claws, standing over a limp, yellow grizzly bear.

"I did that one," Bash said, pointing.

Audrey giggled and then flipped through the pages they hadn't altered to the end. There was a new full spread on a blue wilderness background. Across the top read *Boarlander Second* in big bubble letters, and right under that was a picture of her in the middle of the five guys. They'd taken it when they'd visited her at Moosey's one day, and she was in her work shirt, grinning from ear-to-ear. Bash had bunny ears behind her head, and Harrison's cheek rested against her temple. Kirk and Mason were making goofy faces, and Clinton looked grumpy and was flipping off the camera.

It was perfect.

Beside that was a picture of 1010 with the sun setting behind the mountains in the background. There was a giant cartoon arrow pointing to the trailer that read, *You belong here*. Along the bottom, there were three bear cutouts—a chestnut one, a black one, and a yellow one. Following behind were a gorilla, a white tiger, and a pig. And just above that, there was a question formed with newspaper letters in different shapes, fonts, and sizes. *Will you pledge as a Boarlander?* Below that were two boxes with a *yes* and a *no* written beside them.

Audrey clasped her hand over her mouth and waited until she could compose her face before she looked up at Harrison. She'd dreamed of being officially pledged as a Boarlander since the day she'd fought Clinton.

"Really?" she asked on a hopeful breath.

Lifting his chin proudly, Harrison said, "Everyone who wants to induct Audrey into the crew, say aye."

The ayes were immediate and unanimous. She closed the scrapbook and hugged it to her chest. They'd done this, *her crew*. They'd given her a memento of the best day of her life so far. This was them accepting all of her and securing her place in this park with them for always.

Harrison hooked his finger under her chin and kissed her gently. "What do you say, kitty? You want to be a Boarlander?"

Laughing thickly, she looked at the others, then back to her mate. With a nod, she whispered, "Yes. The answer was always yes."

Harrison hugged her up tight, and she closed her eyes against the bright sun above. She'd lived her entire life on the outside, unable to connect, unable to reveal herself, but that all seemed so long ago now. Her dad had told her once he wanted her to find a place where she felt like she fit. Well, this was it, in an old trailer park nestled deep within Damon's mountains, among a crew of lumberjack shifters, with the man who protected her heart.

Finally, *finally*, she belonged.

Want More of the Boarlanders?

The Complete Series is Available Now

Other books in this series:

Boarlander Bash Bear
(Boarlander Bears, Book 2)

Boarlander Silverback
(Boarlander Bears, Book 3)

Boarlander Beast Boar
(Boarlander Bears, Book 4)

Boarlander Cursed Boar
(Boarlander Bears, Book 5)

About the Author

T.S. Joyce is devoted to bringing hot shifter romances to readers. Hungry alpha males are her calling card, and the wilder the men, the more she'll make them pour their hearts out. She werebear swears there'll be no swooning heroines in her books. It takes tough-as-nails women to handle her shifters.

Experienced at handling an alpha male of her own, she lives in a tiny town, outside of a tiny city, and devotes her life to writing big stories. Foodie, wolf whisperer, ninja, thief of tiny bottles of awesome smelling hotel shampoo, nap connoisseur, movie fanatic, and zombie slayer, and most of this bio is true.

Bear Shifters? Check
Smoldering Alpha Hotness? Double Check
Sexy Scenes? Fasten up your girdles, ladies and gents, it's gonna to be a wild ride.

For more information on T. S. Joyce's work,
visit her website at
www.tsjoycewrites.wordpress.com

Made in United States
Orlando, FL
03 May 2023